HUMPTY BUMPKIN

SAM CHEEVER

Electric Prose Publications

Humpty Bumpkin

Book 1: Country Cousin Mysteries

Published by Sam Cheever

PRAISE FOR SAM CHEEVER

Sam Cheever creates some of the best characters you could ever find in the pages of a book.

— SENSUALREADS.COM

Ms. Cheever writes with class, humor and lots of fun while weaving an excellent story.

— THE ROMANCE STUDIO

She's just a country girl who loves her dog. But her life is about to get less countrified and more...erm...homicide.

Deer Hollow is a small community built in a verdant, rolling countryside. The nearest big city is over an hour away and big city ways are rejected at the Hollow. Unfortunately, the big city isn't the only place where bad things can happen.

Things like murder...which has a funny way of messin' up a debutante's day and turning a sunny Sunday in June right over onto its bucolic head.

CHAPTER ONE

*T*he whole communication revolution thing is a mixed bag of wonderful and tedious. Things like cell phones are a revelation, allowing twenty-something women like me, who have trouble sitting still, to stay in touch with the important people in their lives while we go about our business.

But even the best innovations have their downside.

For example, a wise woman once told me never to answer a phone call whose number you don't recognize. *Answer at your own risk*, my cousin Felicity proclaimed one rainy day in the arboretum.

And I've since witnessed the intelligence of her advice. Several times over.

Unfortunately, I'm apparently a slow learner.

"Hello?"

"Is this Miss Joey Fulle?"

I frowned, not liking the "I want to sell you a bridge" tone of the caller's voice. "Nope, sorry. I think you have the wrong number."

"Actually, I believe I have the right number, Miss Fulle."

"You're not right," I said quickly and disconnected before the man on the other end of the phone had a chance to give me bad news. I had no idea what kind of bad news I was expecting. But I knew it was there, lurking like a vulture in a tree, ugly and ravenous.

I tugged the soft twisty off my shoulder length red-blonde hair and reached up to smooth the hair back into my favorite style, which was a high ponytail. Sweat dripped down between my shoulder blades and I was glad I'd dressed for the heat of an early June morning. Though my plain white tank top and cut off jean short shorts were already damp.

My dog, Cacophony, Caphy for short, bounded up and stopped in front of me, a clump of fur between her jaws. I grimaced. "Caphy, what did you do? Have you killed something again?"

A blonde pit bull with gorgeous green eyes, Caphy bounced several times, her muscular haunches springing her several inches off the ground each time, and then barked happily and ran off again, tail whipping the air. I sighed, knowing I should follow her and see if I could save whatever she'd decided to "play" with.

My phone rang again. I hit *Ignore* and trudged after my dog. "Caphy girl, where'd you go?"

The distant sound of barking drew me to a copse of old trees, their gnarled branches bigger around than I was and tangled together high overhead. It was behind one of these, an elegant old Elm tree whose knobby arms spread wider than the rest, that my dog was mostly hidden. I could see her butt wagging happily as she moved around behind the tree.

"Caphy, come!"

My sweet Pitty bounced out from behind the distant tree and grinned at me, her entire body vibrating with excitement. "What have you found, girl?" I murmured to myself. "Come on, Caphy."

But she turned back to whatever she was exploring. That was when I realized she must have cornered something. I picked up the pace and hurried in her direction.

By the time I was fifteen feet away I smelled something rotting and knew that, whatever she'd found, I wouldn't be saving it.

Real panic set in. "Caphy, you come here right now!"

My dog disappeared behind the tree and I growled with frustration. But a moment later she reappeared, heading in my direction with something hanging out of her mouth. "Ugh!" I fought an impulse to turn and run. Being corpse-woman was not tops on my list of favorite things.

In fact, I was pretty sure it wasn't on the list at all. "Drop it, Cacophony."

Of course she ignored me, her steps becoming bouncier and more excited the closer she came. Clearly she wanted to share her treasure with me. I didn't know how to impress upon her that having a mangled, half dried corpse of a bunny or squirrel dropped on my shoes didn't take me to my happy place. My usual response of shrieking and running screaming away from her treasure just didn't seem to be doing much to teach her.

She was a very bull-headed pitty. I grinned at my pun.

Caphy ran up and dropped to her haunches a few feet away. She kept hold of the object, which I was trying hard not to look at, as if she was afraid I was going to take it away from her. She would be right about that. But it wasn't going to happen until I had a bag or something to use so I didn't have to touch it. I tried one more time to get her to let loose of whatever she was clutching between her jaws. "Drop it, girl." If I was really lucky I could convince her to let go of it and I could drag her home.

To my shock she lowered her head and released the contents of her mouth.

I glanced down. My stomach did a painful little dance and my gag reflex kicked in. Caphy was watching me very carefully, letting the object lie there as if checking to see how I would react. I was glad it was out of her mouth.

4

In fact, I would have been elated about it.

But I was too busy shrieking and running away. It might not work for her...but it worked just fine for me.

~

*D*eputy Arno Willager peered toward the object hulking under the trees. Two, skinny white stick-like things protruded from one end, their bony lengths painted in red streaks. He narrowed his dark brown gaze at the thing, no doubt gawking at the enormous feet on the end of the sticks.

I shuddered beside him, my dog vibrating excitedly next to me on a leash.

"Is this your chipper, Joey?"

I gave him the full force of my hostile blue gaze. "Uh, no, Deputy Willager. It's not my chipper. And, before you ask, that's not my body either."

He lifted a golden eyebrow and quirked wide lips as he skimmed my own personal body a long, slow look. "Oh, I can see that."

I frowned but didn't scold him for giving me the once over. I was on uneven ground with that one because I was pretty sure there'd been one time at a party in high school when I'd been in a closet with Arno, our star quarterback at the time. We'd been pretty drunk and the details of what we'd been doing in there were vague. I decided that changing the subject might be a good idea. "Do you know..." I swallowed hard. "—who it is?"

Arno wrinkled his nose. "Can't be more than a couple people around here with feet that big."

I nodded, covering my nose with a hand as a warm breeze carried the butcher shop stench in our direction. "It's horrible."

Arno didn't respond. Finally, I looked at him. "Did you call Doctor Miller?"

"I did."

"Well that's good." I glanced down at the item on the ground a few feet away. It was part of a hand. A man's hand if size was any indication. The ends of the fingers were missing, and my stomach roiled.

"Tell me how you found it."

"I told you already. "

"Humor me, Joey."

I sighed. "Caphy and I were taking a walk. It's a nice day."

He scoured me a look and I fought a grin. He was just too easy to annoy for his own good. "Caphy ran up ahead and came back with fur in her mouth."

"Fur?"

"Well...I thought it was fur. But clearly it wasn't." My gaze skimmed to the small patch of scalp resting in the dirt where Caphy had dropped it.

"Did you walk up to the chipper?"

"No."

"You didn't touch anything? Move the body parts...?"

"Ew! Of course not. Why would you even ask me that?"

"It's my job."

Frustration twanged my last nerve. Arno had always been a man of few words, but he had to know I had about a thousand questions. As if reading my mind, he turned to frown down at me. The sun dropped slowly behind him, forming a backdrop for his tall, lean frame, narrow hips and broad shoulders. Arno's face was classically handsome, with a clean-shaven square jaw, sexy brown eyes and a pleasantly-shaped mouth with a slightly fuller lower lip that was immensely appealing. Two lines rode the space between his dense golden brows as he looked at me. He was clearly chewing on something he thought he should tell me.

"What is it, Arno?"

The worry lines deepened and he held my gaze with a searching one. "You can't talk about this, Joey. This is an ongoing investigation and I need you to promise me you won't spill details around town."

"I don't know any details."

"You know more right now than anybody else except the killer." He lifted a golden brow for emphasis.

His words finally sank in. "Oh. Yikes."

"I need you to keep a low profile until we figure out what's going on."

"Surely this is someone from outside the *Hollow*."

He shrugged. "We don't know that yet."

I fell silent, chewing my bottom lip as a distant rumbling noise climbed ever closer to the spot where we stood. That would be Doctor Miller and the deputies Arno had called. They would have left their cars on the road and were approaching on all-terrain vehicles. My family's property included well over a hundred acres without roads. And the spot where Arno and I stood was in the most remote section of it all. The killer couldn't have found a more private spot to stick some poor schmoe into a wood chipper.

Finally, I nodded. "Okay. I promise."

"Good. Now you should get on home with that dog. She's disrupted the crime scene enough."

Caphy whined softly and dropped to her wide haunches, plying the deputy with a grin and soft eyes for good measure.

She wrung a grin out of him and he reached out to scratch the wide spot between her eyes. "You're a good girl, Caphy."

My pitty leapt to her feet and started wagging from her nose to the deadly whip of her tail, which unfortunately was smacking painfully against my leg.

I gave her leash a tug and, with one final look at the horror between the trees, we started back toward home. Despite my promise to keep the body in the chipper to myself, I had no intention of doing it. Whoever that poor soul was, he or she was killed on my property.

That made it personal.

And, personally, I didn't like it when people

started flinging other people into wood chippers in my woods.

It was rude and disturbing.

And nipping it in the bud as quickly as possible seemed like the logical thing to do.

CHAPTER TWO

"What do you mean you don't know who it is?" I couldn't believe that, after two whole days Arno didn't seem any closer to finding out who'd been chipped into pieces in my woods. "Have you taken roll call in town?"

"Very funny, Joey."

I frowned. "This is very upsetting."

He sighed. "I know. But I promise you I'm working on it."

"What about dentals?"

"It's kind of hard to reconstruct the pieces."

Argh! "Fingerprints?"

"Chopped."

"I don't suppose he had a wallet in his pocket?"

"If he did I haven't found it. I'm guessing if the killer went to so much trouble to hide the identity of the body, he or she would have made sure to remove any identifying documentation."

I knew he was right. But dang if it wasn't frustrating. "What about the chipper? Where'd it come from?"

"Buck reported it stolen from *Mitzner Landscaping*."

"That's convenient."

"Now Joey..."

"What? I'm just sayin'." Buck Mitzner just happened to be the resident "angry man" in the small town of *Deer Hollow*. He was famous for getting his wick lit over the smallest perceived slight. One time he'd punched a guy at *Sonny's Diner* because the tourist had boasted that the six-point buck he'd shot was the biggest in *Deer Hollow* history.

Buck, whose father had been off deer hunting with friends while his mother was giving birth to infant Buck some fifty years earlier...thus the ill-advised name...figured the biggest buck in Hollow history was already hanging over his own fireplace.

"I wonder if the dead guy's a former client of *Mitzner's*?"

"Joey, I'm looking into it. And you promised me you'd stay out."

"I did, didn't I?"

"Joey..."

"Nothing to worry about, Arno. I made a promise and I'll keep it..." Sort of. "Have a nice day."

I disconnected and quickly dialed my cousin, Felicity.

She answered on the third ring, sounding breathless. "Hey there! How's things in the Hollow?"

"Things have been better."

"Oh?" Felicity sounded immediately concerned. "Are you okay? Caphy?"

"We're both good." I reached down and scratched my dog between the ears, grinning when one of her back legs started to thump with pleasure. "But something's happened in my...erm..."

"Your erm?"

I thought about it for a moment, working out how to technically keep my promise to Arno and still get what I wanted from Felicity. Finally, I went with a pretty standard escape clause. "I have this friend..."

"A friend?"

"Stick with me here. This friend has a hypothetical problem."

"A hypothetical friend with a problem, got it."

"No, the friend isn't hypothetical..." I started to argue, but I recognized that it was all hypothetical. "No, you're right, everything I'm about to tell you is...hypothetical."

"I'm listening."

"This friend was out for a walk with her dog the other day..."

"Was your friend's dog a pibl?"

Joey sighed. "Focus, Felicity."

"Sorry," her cousin's voice throbbed with laughter.

"Anyway, said friend and dog, which may or may

not have been a pit bull, found something horrible in the woods."

"Okay, I'm not liking where this story's going."

"That makes two of us, but my...erm...friend needs help."

"You're in trouble?"

"Not me, my friend. And she's not in trouble so much as, just wanting to get to the bottom of things."

"What things?"

"A dead guy."

Silence throbbed across the phone line. "Dead? How? Why?"

"All TBD, I'm afraid. Well, except for the 'how' part. Think Humpty Dumpty."

"Ew!"

"Yeah. All the King's men are at a loss."

"Joey, please tell me this guy's death isn't somehow tied to you?"

"It's not. Well, I assume it's not. Arno hasn't figured out who it is yet."

"Arno Willager, my favorite villager?"

Joey snickered. "The very one."

"You don't think he can handle this?"

"It's not that. But I definitely think he could use another set of eyes and...skills."

"How can I help?"

"Can I borrow Cal for a few days?" Cal Amity was Felicity's boyfriend as well as a very good Private Investigator. He had a successful Investigation and

Security business in Indianapolis, where he and Felicity lived.

"That might be a problem. Cal's out of town for a few weeks."

"Oh? A new client?"

"Something like that. But I think I can help anyway. His brother's keeping the business alive while he's gone. I can put him in touch with you if you'd like."

"Is he any good?"

"Almost as good as Cal." Felicity laughed. "Better in some ways but don't tell my honey that. Hal's an ex-cop so he's got connections in IMPD. That probably won't help you much down there in the *Hollow*, but his experience as a cop might be just the thing if you're looking to give sexy Arno some unwanted assistance."

"Score. Will you give him my number?"

"I'll do that. Hey, you take care of yourself, okay? I don't like hearing that something so gruesome is going on right under your nose."

"I don't like it either. Hypothetically."

Felicity snorted. "Yeah. Give your hypothetical pibl a kiss for me."

"Will do. Thanks, cuz."

CHAPTER THREE

On a scale of one to ten in the looks department, the man climbing out of the big, black SUV in my driveway was a two thousand and fifty-five. I pressed my nose against the window and stared out at him, almost afraid to approach for fear he was an alien sent to Earth to suck out my brains. He was just too perfect to be real.

Beside me at the window, Caphy licked the glass, pressing her wide, wet nose to the spot and whining sharply.

I knew how she felt. "Don't get too attached, Caphy. I think he's a pod person."

He looked to be about six feet four inches tall, with thick, shiny black hair that was swept straight back from a wide, unlined brow and curled softly at the top of his muscular neck. Dense black lashes framed a pair of sexy dark green eyes and his mouth was full and wide, very kissable. He had a square jaw, with a dimple in the center and broad shoulders under a sport coat and a pristine white tee shirt. The jeans that framed his long, well-shaped legs were just tattered enough to be stylish and the dark brown boots on his feet were scuffed enough to look comfortably broken in rather than just old.

My dog smacked her lips as if she was hungry for pod person. But when the too-sexy alien walked up my front steps and jolted to a stop on my porch, his surprised gaze locking on the idiots with their noses pressed against the glass, she was the first to unpeel her face and run to the door, her entire body wagging.

My gaze found his and locked on, both of us seemingly startled by the unexpected connection.

I quickly backed away from the window, feeling the fool he'd no doubt believe I was.

Caphy's nails clicked and clacked against the hard tile in front of the door as she bounced in happy anticipation of meeting Mr. Gorgeous.

I briefly considered fleeing up the curved staircase and hiding under my covers until he left.

There was a taut silence before his knock thundered through the entryway, bouncing off the twenty-foot-high walls and reverberating against my nerves. I figured he'd hesitated, thinking a knock wasn't necessary since I'd already seen him.

But apparently it was. *I'm such an idiot.*

Wringing my hands, I walked over to the door, took a deep breath, and pulled it open.

Though it seemed impossible, he was even better looking up close. Though individually not perfect... eyes a bit too narrow...nose with a decided bump on the bridge as if it had once been broken...his features worked perfectly well together. His olive skin tone gave him an exotic flavor that made my stomach jump with interest. However, my handsome visitor was saved from being too perfect by the silver line of a razor-thin scar that ran from just in front of his left ear to the corner of his eye.

Unfortunately, that only served to make him seem slightly dangerous. Like crack cocaine to a woman who loves a little bad in her man.

Caphy leapt through the door and wove around his legs like an oversized cat with a whippet tail. Painful sounding smacking noises ensued.

His dark green gaze narrowed slightly as it held mine but he finally looked away long enough to scratch my manic pooch between the ears. "Hey, beauty."

Caphy responded by wagging her entire body and giving him a crazy canine grin.

"She's very shy," I told him on a voice that had gone husky and deep.

He blinked at the sound and I cleared my throat. "Um..." I offered him my hand. "I'm Joey."

His grip was warm and strong. He held my hand a beat longer than necessary and heat blossomed in my belly from the contact. "Hal Amity. It's a pleasure."

You have no idea, I thought before I caught myself.

"Please, come in." I quickly led him away from the window with the grease and slobber spots and into my living room, where I indicated a hard, white couch that was about as inviting as flip flops in mud. "Have a seat. Can I get you anything? Coffee, tea...?" *Every inch of me?*

Hal smiled as if he'd heard my naughty inner voice. "I'm good, thanks. Why don't you fill me in on what's going on?"

I gave a nervous laugh. "Just like that? We're gonna jump right in? Okay."

He tilted his head, creating flashes of blue light from the sun hitting his thick mane of black hair. "You're paying me by the hour. I don't want to waste your money."

"Right." My lustful thoughts died, doused in icy water. His manner was brutal but efficient. "Someone was shoved into a wood chipper in my woods."

He held my gaze, his expression unreadable. I'll admit I was a bit shocked by the non-reaction. Murder by wood chipping was gruesomely efficient even if it wasn't very imaginative.

"Was the victim someone you know?"

"That's the problem. We haven't figured out who it is yet."

Hal inclined his head. "Then you don't know if it's tied to you."

"Exactly."

He looked around the house, his long-lashed gaze

taking in the expensive furniture, pricy paintings and lavish collectibles.

I quickly glanced down at my hands, not wanting to see the judgment I knew would be in his eyes. "My parents died last year. I inherited their house and everything." I shrugged, feeling guilty and then angered because I did. My parents had worked very hard all their lives for what they had. Nobody should feel bad about that. I was aware that others looked at my big home and all the stuff inside and thought less of me because of it.

It had bothered me more since I'd lost them. It seemed like an insult to their memory.

"How did they die?"

"Private plane crash." I didn't elaborate. He didn't need to know about the airstrip out behind the house. Or the chunks of charred and twisted metal that still dotted the center of the now-overgrown grassy stripe. I'd been unable to move forward on removing the wreckage. In fact, I'd pretty much been unable to move forward on anything since that horrible night.

"I'm very sorry for your loss."

He sounded sincere. I skimmed my gaze upward, finding his dark green perusal and seeing the sincerity there.

I shrugged. "Thanks."

He nodded. We sat in silence for a beat. Then he stood up. "Why don't you show me the murder site. You can fill me in on the way."

~

*C*aphy ran on ahead, barking happily at everything that moved. I twisted my fingers together as I picked my way through the woods, stumbling over more objects in my path than I avoided. The third time, when Hal had to catch me so I didn't do a face-plant in the weeds, I got mad at myself. I needed to pull my head out of my butt ASAP. After all, Hal Amity wasn't there for a date. He was there to help me find a killer.

I took a deep breath and forced my mind to the matter at hand.

"So, you wanted to know about the body?"

"Please."

"Caphy and I were walking along this path..."

"What time was it?"

I blinked, surprised out of my narration by the seemingly unrelated question. "Um. Seven thirtyish."

"Early then."

I shrugged. "It wasn't early for me. I haven't been able to sleep past four am since my parents..."

"Do you always walk this same path?"

"I..." Frowning, my thoughts swept past his question looking for a reason behind it. "Well, yes. I guess I do."

"So, someone could have placed the body specifically in a spot where you'd find it."

A flare of alarm sent my pulse rocketing. "I guess they could have, yes."

Up ahead, Caphy reared up and put both paws on a tree, barking excitedly as a squirrel circled the thick trunk on its way to a higher branch.

I looked at Hal. "You think this was meant as a message to me?"

"It's possible."

I chewed the inside of my lip, feeling the beauty of the day sliding away behind a cold and oily menace. "But why? I'm just a country bumpkin in a nice house."

He grinned as if he liked my description. "You're a little more than that though, aren't you? You inherited quite a bit of money when your parents died, along with controlling interest in your dad's company."

I shook my head. "I'm going to give most of that money away as soon as I can figure out who should get it. I don't want it. And I certainly don't care about dad's company. That was his passion. Not mine."

"You've just given me two great reasons for someone to target you."

"I don't understand."

"What if someone was hoping to persuade you to donate to their cause through any means necessary."

I frowned.

"Or, what if someone wanted to get their hands on your controlling interest."

I shook my head, not convinced. "Those are a stretch."

"Agreed. But we need to look at all possibilities here."

"Okay. I get that. But I still think this murder had nothing to do with me."

Caphy reluctantly left the tree and the squirrel behind and bounded on ahead. She stopped and sniffed the ground where the hunk of partial hand had been. I stopped next to her, pointing to the ground. "Caphy dropped a body part here. It was the first inkling I had that something was wrong."

Hal crouched down and eyed the tiny, dark spot in the soil. He lifted his head and looked into the woods, his gaze moving unerringly to the copse of trees that had all but hidden the chipper and its grizzly contents from view.

He stood up and turned in a slow circle. "These ATV tracks, they're from the police?"

I nodded.

"Were there any tracks before they came?"

I thought about his question, realizing for the first time that I hadn't really taken the time to examine the scene before I'd hightailed it out of there. "I didn't notice. Sorry. I was frantic to get Caphy away from the dead body."

"I can certainly understand that." His smile tugged an answering curve of my own lips. "The chipper was over here?" He pointed toward the opening in the trees.

"That's the spot." Hal started to walk that way. "Where's the closest road?"

I stood on the outside perimeter of the spot as Hal walked into the space, stopping just outside the torn-up dirt where the chipper had been. I frowned at the myriad of tracks scarring the ground and wondered what important piece of information I'd missed by acting like a girl and running away.

"Joey?"

I blinked, realizing I'd never answered his question. "Um. Three-quarters of a mile, I guess."

"Which direction?"

"*Goat's Hollow Road*, which is the gravel road that goes past my house, is that way."

"The police came from *Goat's Hollow*?"

"Actually, I think they came from the direction of *Country Road 57*, which leads right into town to the north. It borders my property on the east side."

He nodded and turned away, striding into the woods heading toward *Goat's Hollow*, Caphy on his heels. I was wondering if I should follow them when Hal turned back and motioned for me to come.

As I approached, Hal pointed to the vegetation. "Broken branches, mashed pine needles. Something big's passed through here recently." He crouched down, clearing some of the pine needles. "See here? This is a recreational vehicle track. And that..." he pointed several feet away, "That's a much narrower tire with a relatively shallow tread."

I frowned. "You're thinking these belong to something like an ATV with a chipper on the back?"

"That's what I'm thinking." He stared off into the

woods. "Let's follow this. I'm betting it will come out on *Goat's Hollow Road*."

I fell in with him, my mind spinning. "Deputy Willager said the chipper was stolen from *Mitzner Landscaping*."

Hal threw me a narrow-eyed look. "Willager?"

"Which rhymes with villager...Yes," I told him, grinning.

He flashed me an answering grin before returning to business. "You don't sound like you believe it."

"I didn't when he told me. If I had to pick any one person in *Deer Hollow* who would be capable of killing someone, Buck Mitzner would be at the top of my list."

"Why?"

"He's just one of those people, you know? He yells at everybody. He's always mad about something." I shrugged.

"He'd have to be really stupid to use his own chipper to kill somebody."

"I know. And if the chipper was brought into my woods from this direction, that would put a crimp in my theory anyway."

"Why's that?"

"Mitzner's is north of town. If you headed up *Country Road 57* into Deer Hollow, then continued on through town and out, about a mile on the other side you'd pass it just before you hit the ramp onto Highway 65."

Hal nodded. "This seems to have come from the wrong direction."

"I guess he could have driven around town with it and come in from a different direction to throw us off..."

"But it seems unlikely."

I sighed. "Yeah. It does." A car whizzed past not too far ahead of us and I quickly whistled to Caphy so she didn't run out onto the road. She turned on her heel and ran at us full speed, tongue flapping around her open jaws.

She skidded to a stop in front of me and I reached down to scratch her under her squishy chin. "Good girl." I clipped a lead on her heavy leather collar and we proceeded on to the road.

Hal stopped about ten feet from *Goat's Hollow Road* and nodded. "See the mud tracks there? The ATV crossed the road here."

"Should we keep following it?"

"No need." He pointed to the gravel shoulder on the other side. "I'm guessing they loaded it onto some kind of vehicle there."

I stepped closer and eyed the spot, seeing the tell-tale tracks in the gravel. "I guess we've hit a dead end."

"Not really. If they headed into town, we should be able to pick up their tracks there."

I laughed. "I hope you're not thinking we'll hook up with a computer expert like in one of those cop shows on TV and track their route using traffic cameras. In *Deer Hollow* a *Stop* sign is considered technologically advanced."

Hal gave me a smile that made my toes curl. "You might be surprised what you can find when you go looking." He turned back into the woods. "I'm hungry. How about you?"

As soon as he asked the question my stomach rumbled unhappily. "I could eat."

"Good. I saw a diner in town that looked promising. I'll let you buy me lunch."

I snorted. "Oh yeah? You'll let me?"

"Of course."

I freed Caphy from her leash and Hal picked up a stick, throwing it deep into the woods. She took off like a shot, her entire body vibrating with happy excitement.

"We've already established you're the one with all the money," he said. "Besides, if I'm going to work for you, it makes sense for you to buy me a meal once in a while. You know, to keep me happy so I want to work for you as long as you need me."

I laughed and it felt really good. I liked him. And the realization made the sun warm again on my shoulders. I wasn't alone anymore. I had someone to help me figure out what was going on and to help me stay safe if whatever it was had to do with me.

Caphy burst through the trees ahead, stick firmly clenched between her jaws. She bounced happily toward Hal, clearly anticipating a rousing game of fetch in her future.

I laughed again.

Any man who could make my dog that happy was a man I wanted to get to know better.

And then there was the warm spot he'd caused in the center of my belly. That was just for me.

CHAPTER FOUR

*S*onny's Diner was located in the exact center
of Deer Hollow's main street. If I'm being
honest, it's really the town's only street. The short
spokes of road jutting off either side were little more
than angry outbursts of asphalt and gravel, sporting a
mismatched array of boils along their crooked sides
posing as businesses and homes.

Sonny's real name had been Matthew Earl. He'd
been a selfish, surly only child who was spoiled rotten
by his mother, and she'd called him Sonny his entire
life for no explicable reason.

Sonny's daughter Max was the current owner of
the humble little diner, which squatted under a
massive sign promising the best banana cream pie in
the state.

And it delivered.

My gaze slid to the glass-doored refrigerator
behind the counter as Hal and I entered the diner

and my mouth watered as I saw what was left of the last banana cream pie.

My competitive nature kicked in immediately. It was going be a race to determine who would get that last piece of pie.

A race I intended to win.

I skimmed my glance over the customers in the diner and was happy to see that several of them were either done eating or already had their desserts.

There was only one man I could see who might represent a problem. And I could deal with him.

I headed to the counter and dropped into an oft-taped red vinyl stool that spun around at the slightest movement. I planted my feet on the brass bar running along the bottom of the counter to stabilize myself and waved at the waitress. Verna Bly was down the long counter, waiting on an extremely large man sitting in the last stool.

My competition.

Verna gave me a weary smile and lifted a finger in the universal sign for "don't get your panties in a twist, I'll be there in a minute". Hal slipped into the stool next to mine. "You always sit at the counter?"

My gaze slid over the bulgy form of the beflan-neled farmer giving Verna his order. He shoved at a greasy John Deere hat and scratched the sweat-drenched dark hair underneath. His bulging brown eyes skimmed down the counter and locked onto mine.

He gave me a slow, mean smile.

Verna slid a bored glance my way, a pencil poised over her much-abused order pad. She popped her chewing gum and rolled faded blue eyes, cocking a hip against the counter to wait out the fireworks.

I tightened my lips, giving Bobo Biddens an all-knowing head bob.

His fleshy lips parted, showing a pair of over-sharp canines that looked like they needed a good scrubbing with bleach.

A grinding sound emerged from my jaw.

"Um, Joey?" Hal seemed determined to pull my attention away from my nemesis but I wasn't going to let him. Bobo and I had locked in and we were ready to rumble.

It was on.

I ignored Hal and shook my head once, my gaze turning hard.

Bobo opened his mouth and I saw what he was going to do. He was going to ask for that pie.

"Verna?" I yelled. "Is that your car being towed outside?"

The waitress frowned, running to the front window, her orthopedic shoes slapping against the linoleum.

Seeing his advantage slide away, Bobo showed his teeth in a silent growl. His meaty paw found the counter and the sausage fingers went white as he put weight on it, clearly intending to rise from his stool.

I let my feet slide to the floor, pressing weight into my toes.

I had speed on my side. Bobo had size. If he managed to get to the pie before I did, I would lose.

But I had no intention of letting him get there first.

"Joey, what do you want to eat?" Hal tried again.

I ignored his question.

Lifting my butt from the stool, I slid one hand open on the counter in preparation for shoving off.

A cool breeze wafted over me and something moved in my peripheral vision. A dish clattered to the counter and Hal said something that sounded like "thank you".

Bobo looked murderous. He shoved to his feet so quickly the stool spun wildly behind him.

Looking into his rage-filled eyes, I had a terrible premonition.

No! It couldn't be!

I turned to find Hal shoving a bite of banana cream pie into his face, his expression turning to one of pure rapture. "Mm. This is really good."

I sighed and looked up as a woman with a ratty tangle of yellow-white hair piled on top of her head asked, "What can I get you, honey?"

Max...

I sighed. "I don't suppose you have another slice of that pie hidden in the back?"

"Sorry, Joey. You know it doesn't last very long."

"Yeah." I scoured Hal a hate-filled look. "I do know that."

~

I picked at my salad, my pout firmly in place as Hal followed up the pie I'd wanted with a fat, juicy burger and crispy fries.

I'd ordered the salad in a fit of temper, thinking I'd punish him by making myself miserable. Unfortunately, it didn't occur to me until I'd started eating the dang thing that the only one I'd made miserable was me.

Hal clearly assumed I'd wanted to eat a salad. It was no skin off his Greek nose if I ate like a rabbit while he embraced the role of banana cream pie eating carnivore. "Who was that guy you were glaring at down there?"

"Bobo Biddens."

Hal snorted out a laugh. "You're kidding me, right?"

"I chewed a piece of cucumber and shook my head. "His real name's Pete but everybody calls him Bobo because his last name sounds like Baggins and he generally eats two breakfasts."

Hal grinned around his glass of water. "Elevenses?"

I couldn't help grinning back. "There's a rumor his feet have more hair on them than most people have on their heads."

Hal barked out a laugh and I felt my bad humor oozing away.

"I heard about what happened out at your

place," Max said. She slid a small bowl of something creamy and pale yellow in front of me. It had soggy golden chunks of cookie in it and a big dollop of whipped cream on top. I grinned. "Banana pudding?"

She held a finger up in front of her lips. "I had a bit of filling leftover." She winked and handed me a spoon. "Does Arno know who was killed yet?"

I shook my head and swallowed my first, delicious bite of pudding. "I wouldn't know since he won't tell me anything."

"Yeah, he can be a bit of a prig."

"Arno Willager, our favorite villager?" I asked, feigning surprise.

Max snorted. She leaned her elbows on the counter and spoke in lowered tones. "Rumor is it was a Mitzner chipper?"

I nodded, chewing a thick slice of banana.

"Do you think that's significant?" Hal asked.

She shrugged. "Could be, handsome. Depends who's askin'."

I swallowed. "Sorry. Max, this is my private investigator, Hal Amity."

"PI? Seriously?" The older woman tugged an over-bleached curl from behind her ear and gave him a flirty smile. "You definitely aren't from around here. Indy?"

"Yes, ma'am. My brother and I have an office on the South West side."

She nodded. "Well, since you're helpin' Joey, I'll

tell ya that Buck Mitzner never reported that chipper stolen until after Arno called to ask him about it."

I frowned. Arno had implied that Buck reported it. Still, I didn't want to accuse him of things I couldn't back up. "Really? I got the impression Arno knew about the theft."

Max stared at me a moment as if trying to decide if she was going to let me in on a secret. But after a few seconds she simply shrugged. "Maybe I heard wrong."

"Nobody in town's been reported missing?" Hal asked.

His instincts were good. *Sonny's* was the heartbeat of *Deer Hollow*. If anything was going on in the area, Max usually knew at least something about it. But she shook her head. "Not in town, no. But most of the population lives outside *Deer Hollow*. We have a large number of farmers around here."

"And a few artist types," I added. Dropping my spoon into my empty bowl, I rubbed my napkin over my lips.

"Artist types?" Hal asked. "You mean like painters?"

"A couple people who paint. One sculptor. And I think we have two writers too," I told him. "A couple are kind of famous."

He thought about that for a moment. "That seems like a lot of artist types for one rural area."

It was my turn to shrug. "You wouldn't say that if

you'd seen the area. It's beautiful around here pretty much year-round."

Max nodded enthusiastic agreement.

"I get the impression you don't completely trust Deputy Willager," Hal said to Max.

She shook her head. "It's not that I don't trust him. I've known that boy since he was a baby. I changed his diapers for gosh sakes. He's a good person and a decent cop. But he tends to get caught up in loyalties and he don't see that people have a dark side."

I frowned. She was right. But I wasn't comfortable seeing that dark side myself. "I guess that's a side effect of living somewhere all your life. Knowing everybody."

Max patted my hand. "Good luck, honey. I have a feeling with this one's help you're gonna find your killer."

~

*M*itzner's Landscaping was the largest greenhouse and landscaping store and service within sixty miles of *Deer Hollow*. Buck Mitzner ruled the business with an iron and acerbic hand, running through employees like poop through a goose. But despite his harsh manner with his people, he knew more about the business than anyone else, even as far as Indianapolis, and he drew business from all around the state.

Plus, he was one of the biggest employers in Southern Indiana, which made his tendency to run off the faint of heart little more than a nuisance. The turnover was mostly a problem for his office manager, Cindy Pickett. Buck just broke 'em, he didn't fix 'em. But Cindy, who attended the same gym I did several times a week, confided in me once that she'd gotten good at creating employment queues, basically hiring the next employee about a week after the first one started, knowing that, by the time they got through the paperwork and pre-employment testing, the first one would be haring it toward the door with tears of rage making tracks down their cheeks.

Heck of a way to do business.

I climbed out of Hal's government-type SUV and stood looking around. It occurred to me that I should probably stop procrastinating on replacing the dead bushes around my house. I'd been meaning to do it for months, but somehow I'd never worked up any enthusiasm for the task.

Maybe it was time to start that process. Or at least, begin a conversation about it with the man striding quickly in my direction.

I skimmed Hal a quick glance. "Let me do the talking."

He frowned slightly. I took that as agreement because I wanted to.

Pasting a smile on my face, I approached the tall, gray-haired black man with an outstretched hand.

"Miss Joey. How are you, child?"

My smile might have started out fake, but it quickly grew genuine as my hand was enveloped in Marcus Callum's big, warm grip. I could feel the callouses on his palms as he clasped my hand, and pleasure filled me in a warm rush as he beamed down at me. His brown gaze was filled with genuine affection. "I'm good, Marcus. How have you been? I haven't seen you in church lately." Truth was, I hadn't been in church lately either. I was just tweaking him a little.

He winked at me. "With all my sinnin' and wild ways, the Lord like ta pull that building down around my big ears if I step through that door, child. You know that."

I twisted my lips against a grin. "You're terrible. And I happen to know you'd be more likely to see sainthood than lightning bolts if you went to services."

He laughed. "Child, you been drinkin' your bathwater again?"

I felt Hal stiffen as I chuckled. "I told you, bath salts are a drug, not the real thing."

"That's good. 'Cause I'm mighty partial to some *Epsom* in my tub. I'd hate ta think if I slipped and swallowed a bit I'd start eatin' people's faces."

Shaking my head, I asked, "How's Mary?"

"Sour as a lemon and pretty as a rose."

"So...normal?" I said with a grin.

He chuckled. "What can I help y'all with today?

You finally gonna replace them dead bushes up by your house?"

"I am, actually. I'd love your help with that. But there's something else..."

Marcus's face folded into a frown. "I heard about the murder." He reached out and touched my arm. "That didn't have nothin' ta do with you, did it?"

"I don't think so," I told him, biting my lip. "But you can understand how I'd be a little nervous, since it was on my property."

"Of course." Crossing his arms, Marcus leaned back against a pretty arbor with fat purple clematis blossoms climbing thickly over its frame. "I'm sure somebody just picked an out-of-the-way spot and it had nothin' ta do with you, Miss Joey."

"Maybe..."

"We won't know that for sure until the body's identified," Hal put in.

Marcus turned to Hal, his face creasing in a tense smile. "And who is this fine gentleman?"

"This is Hal Amity. He's helping me figure out what's going on."

Marcus's smile gained another level of tense. "You a cop?"

"No, sir," Hal answered respectfully. "I'm a private investigator."

"He's the brother of Felicity's friend, Cal."

Understanding lit Marcus' gaze. "Ah. How *is* your pretty cousin these days?"

"She's great. She sounds really happy."

"She ever find that daddy of hers?"

I gave him a secretive smile. "Of course not, Marcus. If she had, she would have told the government where he was." I winked and he chuckled darkly.

"Course she would. Well, any friend of Joey's and Felicity's is a friend of mine." He offered Hal his hand. "Welcome ta *Deer Hollow*."

Hal shook his hand, grimacing a bit as Marcus no doubt gave him a warning squeeze. I had no idea how old Marcus was, but he'd been a fixture in *Deer Hollow* for as long as I could remember so I knew he was up there in years. Still, he seemed sturdy and was only slightly stooped around the shoulders. I suspected he was strong enough to take care of business when it was required.

"The police said the chipper used in the murder came from *Mitzner's*," Hal told the other man.

Marcus flinched as if struck. "You don't say?"

"It's true," I told him. "Buck reported it stolen. Do you know when it was taken from the lot?"

Marcus narrowed his gaze at me and then swung it to Hal. "Stolen? First I heard of it." He shook his head. "But don't read nothin' into that. Buck don't tell me anything."

I could believe that. I'd seen the two men together and it was clear they didn't get along. Marcus had proclaimed once that he was too stubborn to let Buck's nasty nature run him off a good job...one he loved...and Buck often looked at his employee like he was peeved he couldn't scare him away.

"Can we see where the chippers are kept?" Hal asked.

Marcus shook his head. "Sorry, son. But we don't have any right now. We had three but one's on loan to the Johnstons out off *Baileyville Road*. The other's in the shop. Broken blades or some such."

"And the third one's with the police," Hal said.

Marcus nodded. "Yeah. I guess so. I figured Buck had rented it out to somebody."

"How do you know which is which?" I asked.

"They're all numbered," Marcus responded. "When we rent one out we write the number on the paperwork so we can keep track."

"That makes sense," I told him with a smile.

"Horrible way to go," Marcus murmured, almost to himself.

"It is," I agreed.

"Is Mr. Mitzner here?" Hal asked.

Marcus' gaze shot to the PI, filled with surprise. "Yeah. He is. But he's leavin' soon. He's got to go talk to the Reverend about replacin' those hydrangea bushes around the front of the church."

Hal offered Marcus his hand. "Thanks for your help."

The other man clasped it and almost immediately winced as Hal, no doubt, returned the favor.

I grinned behind my hand.

"I'm not sure I helped but, you're welcome,"

Marcus responded. "I don't want to see Miss Joey get hurt."

"I'll make sure that doesn't happen, sir," Hal promised.

Okay, I'll admit it. I was feeling a little tingly over that promise as I headed for Mitzner's Store.

CHAPTER FIVE

*B*uck Mitzner was helping a customer when we entered the building. A bell jangled brightly overhead and Buck looked up from the receipt he was hand writing and glowered at us. I skimmed Hal a look and he gave me back cop face.

The woman Buck handed the receipt to thanked him cheerily and turned, blinking in surprise when she saw me. "Joey Fulle! How are you?" She grabbed me up and pulled me into a hug.

To my eternal shame, I hadn't seen the woman for almost two years. Not since before my parents were killed. She was the mother of my best friend from high school. "Hi, Mrs. Villa. How's Lis doing? I haven't seen her for months."

"She's just fine, dear. She's loving Indianapolis. But she'll be home in a couple of days for a visit. You should drop over and see her."

"I'll try to do that," I said, non-committal. She

reached out and clasped my hand, her smile turning down. "I heard what happened. Are you all right? Do you need a place to stay?"

I shook my head. "I'm okay. Really. But thanks so much for asking."

Mrs. Villa nodded, her dark blue gaze sliding to Hal and filling with speculation. She gave him a bright smile, offering him her hand. "Hello. I'm Nancy Villa."

Hal took the hand and shook it, returning her smile. "Hal Amity. It's nice to meet you."

I could tell Mrs. Villa was very curious about Hal, but Buck was moving around behind the counter as if he was getting ready to bug out and we needed to talk to him before he left. "Tell Lis I'll call her, okay?"

"I will. You take care now, honey."

I headed toward the counter, Hal dropping into my wake.

Buck looked up and frowned as I approached the counter. He was generally a surly person, but he seemed even more unhappy to see me than usual. "Hey, Buck."

He didn't respond. Instead, he skimmed a look at Hal. "I told the police everything there is to know."

Hal pushed past me, offering Buck his hand. "Mr. Mitzner. I'm Hal Amity. I'm here at the behest of Miss Fulle's cousin. The family believes she needs protection."

Buck's frown deepened and his face folded into a scowl.

I fought a grin. In one smooth statement, Hal had reminded Buck that he wasn't the only one affected by the murder. "We just wanted to ask about the chipper, Buck. When was it stolen?"

He shoved a stack of receipts under the tray in the old-fashioned cash register and slammed it closed. "Like I told Arno, it was a few days ago."

"Was the chipper on the lot when it was taken?" Hal asked the owner.

Buck's gaze slid downward, evading Hal's direct stare. "Uh. Yeah. Around back."

"Do you have security cameras back there?"

Buck snorted. "I know it must be hard for you city slickers to believe, but the world outside of Gomorrah isn't draped in cameras that spy on people. This is the country, son. We enjoy true freedom from snoops here."

"Security isn't a dirty word, Mr. Mitzner."

I almost laughed. Hal would never sell that notion around *Deer Hollow*. Our town motto was, "what you see is what you get and if you try to steal it you'll be chewing on the business end of a rifle before you can say, Miranda rights."

"Snooping in other folks' business sets a bad precedent," Buck told him with a glance toward the door. "Nothin' good ever comes of it."

"There's a body over at the hospital morgue that would probably disagree with you, Mr. Mitzner."

Buck flinched. "If that's all, I got someplace to be."

44

"Buck, please. Hal isn't wrong. The murder on my property has got me spooked. We're just trying to figure out who was in the chipper so I'll know if I need to be worried."

"Why would you need to be worried, little girl?" Buck's voice had gone soft, suspiciously friendly.

I shrugged. "What if the killing was some kind of message?"

"About what? Have you been using the wrong hair product? Did you steal a pair of shoes out from under someone's hand at *Barley's* last shoe sale?"

My eyes burned with unshed tears. I'd always suspected he had a low opinion of me. But having it thrown in my face was hard to swallow. "I actually do have real-life concerns just like everybody else, Buck. I'm not just an empty-headed twenty-four-year-old."

He grabbed a notebook off the counter. "Like I said, I need to be somewhere." He stared at us until I spun on my heel and we left the store.

But we didn't leave the lot. By mutual, silent agreement, Hal and I sat in Hal's car and watched the store until Buck came out a few minutes later. He locked the front door and, giving the lot a quick scan, hurried to his truck and wasted no time jumping into it.

The store owner left a cloud of gravel dust behind as he drove out of the lot.

"He's hiding something," I told Hal.

"Yes, he is." Hal reached for the door handle.

"Where are you going?" I asked him.

"To look around back." He bent down to look through the door at me. "You coming?"

The space behind the flower building was dotted with piles of gravel and mulch. Weeds grew up along the building and in the areas between the piles. There was an open stretch about fifteen feet from the building and it sported unmistakable signs of having held something mechanical. The rock was rusty in spots, coated in black oil in others, and showed evidence of tire tracks leading away from the oily areas.

Hal examined the space carefully before glancing my way. "There were clearly three of something parked here. I have no doubt they were chippers like Marcus said." He frowned.

"But?"

He lifted his head, scanning the roofline of the nearby building. "I was really hoping there'd be security cameras."

I shook my head. "I'm afraid you're going to be continually disappointed if you don't disabuse yourself of that notion, Hal."

He nodded. "I'll try." Throwing me a grin, he jerked his head toward the car. "Let's go."

～

*H*al pulled his SUV into my long, winding driveway. He'd been thoughtful all the way home. As we climbed the final hill toward the house, he turned to me. "What do you know about the Johnstons?"

I shook my head. "They're a dead-end for us. I think Mr. Johnston's probably close to eighty and she's not much younger. I don't see either of them shoving a body into a chipper and dumping it in my woods. Even if they had a reason for doing it they're not physically capable."

"But they rented a chipper."

"Mr. Johnston likes to chop up sticks in the yard. But nothing bigger than my wrist. It's not them."

As we neared the house, it suddenly occurred to me that he was going to need a place to stay. "Have you gotten reservations in town yet?"

"Not yet."

Something about the way he said it gave me pause. "You're not driving back to Indy, are you?"

"I'd thought about it."

I turned away from him, my teeth worrying my bottom lip. I'd only known him for a few hours and purely on a business basis. His and my relationship was bereft of emotion and stripped of personal connection. Yet I felt as if he had quickly become the shield between me and the horror of my situation and I didn't want him to leave.

"You can stay at the house if you'd like. It's a huge house and there's only Caphy and me."

His handsome face altered slightly and I suddenly knew without a doubt that he would say no. I fought a jolt of panic at the knowledge.

"Looks like you have company."

My gaze jerked upward and I saw the big, black car parked before my front door. A man stood on the wide, covered porch, his medium-sized frame wrapped in an ill-fitting dark suit and his face made unrecognizable behind dark sunglasses. His sandy-brown hair was combed from a side part and looked as if it was glued into place. His red tie was too short, his sleeves just a titch too long. "Men in Black," I murmured, thinking that if the man on my porch wasn't government, I'd eat some of Caphy's kibble.

Hal nodded, his expression stoic.

"I wonder who it is."

"We're about to find out," he told me as he pulled around the circular drive and parked behind the visitor's car.

I looked at the stern expression and the stiff stance of the man who turned toward us, moving slowly down the steps with his hands held loosely at his sides as if he were ready to draw a gun.

Something ugly rolled in my chest. I recognized it as fear. "I don't like the looks of him," I told Hal.

He inclined his chin and turned to me. "You stay in the car. Let me speak to him first."

I felt like a coward but I did as he asked because my instincts were screaming at me to run. As Hal opened his door my hand snaked out without my conscious approval and latched onto his arm with desperation. "Be careful."

His smile should have made me relax. He emitted

an unconcerned vibe...a wave of confidence that would have been soothing if the man standing at the bottom of the steps hadn't already pulled his coat open to show me a gun in a holster across his chest.

I swallowed hard.

The man fixed me with a hard look, ignoring Hal as he unfolded his long, intimidating length from the car. I understood in that moment, when the visitor's dark, hostile gaze met mine, that Hal wasn't going to save me from my fate.

Whatever that fate might be.

"Miss Fulle, you need to step out of the car, please."

I gulped again because I recognized the voice.

It was the voice from the phone calls. And I didn't like it better coming directly from the source, than I had when it had simply been a disembodied threat on the phone.

CHAPTER SIX

*H*al stepped between the man and me, blocking him from my view. His hand slipped around to his back and lifted his shirt, and I felt my eyes go wide as I spotted the gun he'd stuffed there.

I reached for the door handle as panic flared. I couldn't let Hal do something we all might regret. Not because I was too much of a sissy to step out and face whoever was standing on my drive.

I opened the door and launched myself out of the car. "Hal!"

He didn't look my way. "Get back in the car, Joey."

"No." I hurried around the front of the SUV and placed my hand on his arm, stopping him from pulling the gun. "That's not necessary."

His gaze was locked on the other man, unwavering and smoldering with hostility. The muscles under my fingers were rock hard. In the blink of an eye, my easy-going PI had transformed back into the cop he'd once been. I suddenly realized he would have been an excellent cop.

He certainly had the attention of the gun-toting intruder. That man had pulled off his government-issue sunglasses and his dark, beady gaze was locked on Hal, his jaw hard. "This is none of your business, Mr. Amity."

I flinched but Hal showed no signs of being surprised that the other man knew his name. He either had a consummate poker face or he knew the guy. "If you want to speak to Miss Fulle you need to hand me that gun first."

The man gave his head a quick shake. "That's not going to happen."

From inside the house, Caphy's joy-filled greeting had changed as thoroughly as Hal's demeanor. The happy chirp of her welcoming bark had turned deep, more growl than bark, and she was flinging herself repeatedly at the door, desperate to get to me. "Both of you stand down. You're scaring my dog."

The man with his back to my front door flinched as the wood creaked under her dense, muscular weight and he half turned to make sure she was still safely contained. "Miss Fulle, I need you to come with me. I need to ask you some questions."

I didn't hesitate. "I'm not going anywhere with you. And we're going to start by you answering some questions of mine. Like, for instance, who are you?"

Caphy slammed against the door again and the frame rattled. The man twitched, his eyes going wide. "I don't want to hurt your dog…"

"You hurt a hair on that dog and you'll be eating dinner through your butt," Hal growled. In that moment I didn't know which of my protectors was more dangerous. I only knew that I'd put money on either one of them over the guy standing in front of us.

"Give Hal the gun. You have no reason to worry about us, but from where we stand we have all sorts of reasons to worry about you. And I won't be answering any questions until you do it."

Caphy slammed against the window and I heard a crack. I looked at Hal. "She's going to break through and hurt herself."

The other man didn't like the sound of that. He quickly lifted his hands in the air. "I'll give you my gun. Just call off that beast."

I glared at him, stepping around him as he handed the gun to Hal with two fingers. I unlocked my front door and slipped inside, dropping to my knees so Caphy could reassure herself that I was all right. After a moment of frantic face kisses, her tail snapping loudly against the wall and whining sounds of concern coming from her thick throat, I grabbed her leash from the table beside the door and snapped it on. "Be still," I told her in my serious voice and she dropped to her haunches beside me, her tongue lolling happily.

I opened the door and fixed Hal with a look, giving him a quick nod. "You might as well come on in. It's hot out there. I have fresh lemonade in the refrigerator."

The man narrowed his gaze at Caphy and her dense throat rumbled in a low growl. "Be still, girl."

She stopped, but her pretty green gaze locked on him, her body vibrating with angry excitement. I turned away from the door and walked to the kitchen, Caphy smashed against my side.

I didn't look to see if the men followed. Hal wouldn't come inside without the other man. And there was no way either of them was leaving.

I had to admit I was curious now that the voice on the phone had intruded on my life. Clearly, he wasn't just an annoying junk caller. He smelled like government goon to me.

And that meant whatever he was there about, it wasn't good. All the doubts I'd wrestled with from the time I was old enough to know I should be worried resurfaced. I'd thought I was done with them when my parents' plane had taken a nosedive in our back acreage. I should have known better.

I was aware of when the man entered the kitchen because Caphy's big body stiffened and a low rumble filled the air. I didn't correct her again. It wouldn't hurt the man to understand what he was dealing with.

Besides, Hal had the man's gun. He couldn't do her any harm.

I placed an icy glass of freshly squeezed lemonade on the counter of my island and nodded toward the stools. "Sit. Talk."

He sat but he didn't reach for the lemonade. His gaze was locked on my dog.

Hal walked around the island and stood next to me, Caphy between us. I handed him a lemonade and he took a long swig from it, his hand dropping to scratch my dog between her ears.

Finally, the man must have realized there was only one way to get to the end of the present stand-off. And that was to push right through it. He frowned, dropping his hands to the countertop and staring at them for a moment before he started to talk.

"I'm Special Agent Richard Cox with the Criminal Investigation Division of the FBI."

I blinked in surprise. "*Criminal* Investigation? Why are you pestering *me*?"

He slipped his hand into the inside pocket of his coat and pulled out a badge, flipping it open for us to view.

Hal leaned in and examined it closely. "Why is the FBI harassing a private citizen?"

The man eyed Caphy before giving Hal a snotty smile. "Investigating, Mr. Amity. Not harassing."

"Funny," I said, "it feels like the same thing to me."

Cox shrugged. "I wouldn't have had to come here in person if you'd spoken to me on the phone one of the twelve times I called."

Hal skimmed me a look, his brows lifting.

I looked quickly away. "I don't take junk calls."

Cox shook his head. "I need to talk to you about your parents."

I went very still, my body turning to rock. Beside me, Caphy whined, jumping to her feet. Her worried gaze rose to mine and she gave my thigh a lick. I reached down and rubbed a hand over her soft head, wondering if I could get out of the kitchen before somebody stopped me.

"Miss Fulle?"

"My parents are dead, Mr. Cox. They couldn't have done anything for you to investigate. It's time the government left them alone, don't you think?"

"I'm sorry for your loss," he said softly, catching me off guard. "But, although your parents are gone, the results of their efforts are still very much alive."

Hal crossed his arms over his chest. "What results?"

I looked at him and frowned, giving my head a quick shake.

He frowned back.

"Miss Fulle, I don't think you want Mr. Amity here for this conversation."

I bit my lip, unsure if he was right. The last thing I wanted to do was air my family's dirty laundry with Hal. I couldn't bear to see the look of doubt or even pity in his eyes when he learned about my shady past.

Sensing my distress, Hal turned to Cox, taking the heat off me. I could have hugged him for it. Hal stared at the special agent for a moment and then addressed me without glancing my way. "I'll be right outside the door if you need me."

It was all I could do not to grab his hand and hold him there. My fingers even flicked toward his, but in the end, I was more humiliated by the idea of him finding out, than I was afraid of being alone with Cox.

The agent waited until Hal strode out of the room before turning to me. "I'm sorry, Miss Fulle. I know this is hard. I want you to understand that the FBI is sensitive to your pain..."

"Cut the crap, Cox," I told him in a voice that made Caphy growl softly. Her gaze never left him and her densely muscled form was rigid against my leg. I might sometimes be confused about who the good guys and the bad guys were in my life, but my dog never doubted for a moment that I was to be protected at all costs and the man facing me across my own kitchen was the devil straight from Hell.

I loved her for that.

Cox threw Caphy a worried look and then adopted a placating tone. "It's not your fault, Miss Fulle. We know that. But, unfortunately, your parents have put you in a difficult spot. You're the only one who can help us make this right."

"Make what right, exactly."

I wasn't playing with him. Though I'd suspected from the time I was old enough to use rational thought, that my parents might be mixed up in something that wasn't exactly on the up and up, I never knew what that something was. And the one time I'd found the courage to ask, I'd made my father so angry I wasn't sure he'd ever forgive me for it. I'd learned nothing and I'd fought with the man who'd always had my back. The one man I could always count on to take up for me and love me unconditionally. Only I wasn't sure if I'd betrayed that love...breaking the one rule he could never forgive.

He'd died before I could make things right.

And now Special Agent Cox was asking me to put a fork in my father's memory, creating even more harm to him in his death.

"You're aware your parents were involved in smuggling."

I jerked as if slapped. "That's a lie!"

Caphy growled, surging to her feet.

"I'm sorry to upset you," he said, glancing worriedly at my dog. "But there's little doubt of it."

"Where's your proof? You people hounded them incessantly for the last two years of their lives. You threatened and accused and made our lives a living hell. But there were no charges, Special Agent Cox. Why was that? If you had proof you would have charged them."

"Miss Fulle..."

"Isn't that true, Agent Cox?"

He looked down at the counter, his jaw tight. "We need your help."

"My help?" I shrieked. "You want me to help you

destroy the only thing my parents have left in this world? Their reputations...their trusted place in this town's history?" I shook my head. "Get out of my house."

Cox rose to his feet. "I don't want to do this the hard way." All cajoling was gone. In the place of his formerly understanding demeanor was the jerkish exterior we'd seen outside.

"Do your worst, Cox. I know you will anyway. I've seen how your kind operates. I haven't done anything wrong and you have no proof they did anything wrong either. Now leave before I release my dog to escort you out."

Of course I was bluffing. I wouldn't risk Caphy's safety by releasing her. She'd definitely show the agent her displeasure about his being in our home and he'd make sure she suffered for it.

He wasn't worth any pain he might cause her.

Hal stepped through the door. "Let's go, Agent Cox. I'll show you out."

Cox threw me one last, angry glance before leaving. I hadn't seen the last of him. As soon as he left the kitchen my knees buckled and I slumped to the ground, my legs splayed out in front of me and my back against the cabinet beneath the sink. Caphy dropped down next to me and laid her head on my thigh, whimpering softly.

I scratched her ears and stared straight ahead, my hands shaking with emotion.

When Hal returned, he slid down to sit on the

floor across from me, his broad back resting against the island. He waited until I scraped the tears from my cheeks and pulled air into my lungs. "I can't explain it to you. Not yet. I need time to come to grips with it myself."

He nodded. "No problem. What can I do to help?"

I thought about it for a long moment and then sniffed, shoving to my feet. "Come on."

He grabbed Caphy's leash from me when he saw how badly my hands were shaking. "Where are we going?"

"To visit a friend I haven't seen in a while." It wasn't strictly a lie. Devon Little had been a family friend for as long as I could remember. The fact that he'd worked for my parents didn't change that. I'd called him Uncle Dev for much of my life. But I'd seen him only once since my parents' funeral. I'd run into him by accident in town and he'd gotten away from me as quickly as he could.

I was pretty sure he wouldn't want to see me again. Though I couldn't explain why that would be. I'd assumed he didn't like the reminder of my father, his lifelong best friend, that I gave him. But it was time for him to get past the pain.

Just like it was time for me to face the ghosts of my past. And finally put my parents' sins to rest. Whatever they might be.

CHAPTER SEVEN

*U*ncle Dev lived in a ramshackle cabin deep in the woods. His property adjoined ours on the south side, a long, barbed wire fence severing one plot from the other. Though our properties were geographically close, separated by only a mile of road, they were miles apart in levels of habitability.

Where my parents had built an imposing home, an enormous fixture anchoring the center of a hundred acres of parklike grass and trees with a small pond nearby, Devon Little had left his heavily treed property wild and untamed, like his own nature. Uncle Dev had been a child of nature for as long as I could remember.

In fact, one of his favorite hobbies had been sitting outside and summoning the coyotes by mimicking their calls. I'd once asked him why he did it and he'd told me it gave him a feeling of being at one with nature when those beautiful, deadly and wild creatures emerged from the woods, one by one, and stood looking at him.

I secretly suspected he fed them and that was why they came. But he vehemently denied it.

The access road to Dev's home at the very back of the property was narrow, rutted and less gravel than roots and weeds. Enormous trees crowded the narrow road, their limbs brushing the top and sides of Hal's car as we lumbered slowly along.

The road stopped a couple of miles in without any warning. The trees barring our way looked as if they'd been there for years, though I remembered the road reaching all the way to his cabin when I was a child.

Hal hit the ignition button and sat staring at the trees. "I guess we're on foot the rest of the way."

I climbed out, secretly relieved to put off the meeting with my errant "uncle" for a while longer. It had been too long and his sad face brought back too many distressing memories.

A shock of realization hit me as I let Caphy out of the back seat. Apparently, Dev wasn't the only one who was afraid to face the pain of those memories.

Hal gave me the gift of silence as we walked more deeply into Devon Little's property. His presence beside me comforted but didn't intrude. I really liked that about him. I'd never met a man quite like Hal Amity.

By contrast, my dog was an occasional blur in the near distance, her wide body bounding lightly over weeds and through scrub trees with happy exhilaration. She ran with her nose down mostly, only lifting it to observe a bird chirping high above her head or the panicked scramble of a squirrel bounding from tree to tree.

Not for the first time, I wished I could see life through her eyes. Though Caphy had been a badly mistreated puppy when I got her, abandoned, starving, and covered in mange alongside the road, she'd accepted my love with a sweet nature that seemed impossible given her early life.

I'd had Caphy only a couple of years before my parents had died. And when I lost them, she was the only thing tethering me to life. I'd wanted to curl up beneath my covers and go to sleep after the crash. I had no desire to eat or move or talk to anyone.

Caphy had laid beside me for two days, only leaving when a friend or relative came to drag her out for food, or a potty break. But then she apparently decided I'd given in enough to my grief and she'd pestered me incessantly to leave the bed.

Only her bright, happy insistence to celebrate life had dragged me from my bed. Nothing or no one else could have done it. To this day I felt like she'd saved my life and my love for her was as fierce as any emotion I held dear.

Even my memories of my parents.

I shook off the memory of those horrible days and turned to Hal. "He'll be armed and he'll probably threaten to shoot us."

Hal blinked but quickly schooled his expression. "I thought you said he was your uncle."

I'd given him a brief explanation of my relationship with Dev on the ride over.

"He's my godfather and a family friend. But he was more my father's friend than mine, of course. And he's become little more than a hermit since my parents' death."

Hal nodded, frowning in thought. A moment later he slowed to a stop and put out an arm to hold me back. He listened carefully for a moment and then slid me a look. "Call Caphy back."

Something much bigger than a rabbit rustled the underbrush about twenty yards away and my pulse picked up.

Fear razored through me but I did as he asked, giving a quick, high-pitched whistle. Silence followed my summons so I whistled again.

I was just starting to panic when I saw her blonde form bounding toward us through the woods. She burst from the underbrush with a happy smile, which was broken in the middle by a slash of grayish-white.

Dread cut a path through my belly. "Is that what it looks like?"

Hal glanced quickly around before crouching down and eyeing the bone in Caphy's mouth.

I didn't breathe for a long moment and then he put out his hand and my dog obediently dropped the offensive object into it. He examined it quickly and then stood, flinging it high and long into the brush.

Caphy turned and ran after it, her entire back end wagging blissfully. "Um, do you think that was a good idea?" I asked Hal.

He grinned. "It wasn't human. It was deer, if I'm not mistaken. Does Uncle Devin hunt?"

I nodded, filled with relief. "He does. And there are a lot of coyotes around here."

"Good to know. I won't throw the bone so far next time."

Three moderate flings of the deer bone later, we came upon a clearing and I stopped as memory swamped me. I couldn't believe how much the place had changed. While his home had never been fancy or even pretty, Devon had always kept the little cabin tidy and in good repair.

No longer.

The glass in the front door was broken, repaired with duct tape and so filthy it looked opaque. The window was cracked, the frame rotting away from the wall, and birds had created nests under the eaves and on top of the crooked gutters.

The roof had been patched, badly, and several of the shingles were obviously buckling. An ugly wash of black mildew covered the once light-brown surface.

The still I remembered squatted at the edge of the woods. I almost smiled as I remembered him telling me when I was eight years old that it was a lemonade cooker. That particular fairytale came to an abrupt end one day when I took a big swig of his home-made "lemonade" and puked it out all over the floor of his cabin.

That was the first time I could remember Dev and my father fighting.

"It doesn't look like he's here," Hal said.

Caphy whined at the front door, scratching the weathered wood and sniffling around the cracks in the glass when her summons wasn't immediately answered.

"You could be right. If he was here he'd have drawn down on us by now."

"That's not healthy," Hal offered unhelpfully.

"Right? I used to tell my dad that all the time."

"Did he know why your uncle was so nervous?"

I shrugged. "He said Devon had always been that way. That he was just a really private person."

Hal tried looking in the window but a stained and ratty curtain covered most of the glass. I went to the door and knocked, peering through the crack in another curtain to see if he was there. Hal joined me at the door and I shook my head. "No lights. Nothing moving inside."

Hal reached for the door and twisted the handle. It turned easily and the door came open. It wasn't locked.

He glanced at me. "A nervous, really private person who doesn't lock his door?"

My eyes went wide and my pulse picked up. "Something's wrong."

"Stay here," Hal whispered harshly. He reached

down and grabbed Caphy's collar, pulling her away from the door. "Keep her with you, just in case."

I clipped Caphy's leash on and whispered a command for her to sit. She did as commanded, though her tail smacked against my leg as she watched Hal disappear into the darkened cabin.

I chewed my lip as silence beat around me. Caphy whined softly.

A moment later, Hal reappeared. "He's not here. But the place is a mess."

I followed him back inside, keeping Caphy close as I stepped into the main room. "Somebody tore the place up," I breathed.

Furniture was slashed and smashed into slivers. Pillows had been reduced to puffs of stuffing and strips of fabric, and every drawer in the place had been yanked out and turned upside down on the floor. "What would they have been looking for?"

Hal crouched down near the closet and reached to tug a couple of coats off the floor. He glanced up as I moved near, his eyebrows lifting. "Wherever your uncle is, he's not armed."

Devon's shotgun lay across the floor of the closet.

"He kept it propped up behind the door," I told Hal. "What was it doing in here?"

Hal stood, shrugging his shoulders as if trying to slough off a burden. "He might have been hiding in here when whoever did this arrived."

We turned and looked around and that's when I

saw the trail of blood across the floor. It led to the front door.

Hal pulled out his phone. "He might have shot the intruder."

I bit my lip as he punched the numbers 9-1-1 into his cell and told the dispatcher where we were. I couldn't shake the fear that Devin might not have shot the intruder. He might have gotten shot himself.

Hal disconnected and clasped my arm, drawing me gently toward the door. "We need to wait outside. This is a crime scene now."

⁓

I'd always thought Arno was tall. If I hadn't seen him standing next to Hal Amity, his head a couple of inches below the other man's, I'd probably still think he was tall.

Everybody looks tall when you're only five feet three inches high.

Caphy and I sat on a filthy wood bench near the still, watching as Arno's guys swarmed all over the tiny cabin. Caphy had given up trying to go to Hal and lay in the shade, her body flat against the ground but her eyes locked on my PI.

A moment later, Hal said something to Arno and they headed my way. Caphy leaped up and gave them a welcoming smile, tongue lolling and tail snapping against the bench.

One of these days she was gonna break that poor tail smacking it against everything.

Arno inclined his head, giving my dog a quick scratch between her ears. "Joey."

"Any idea where Dev is?" I asked him as I stood.

"No. He hasn't been into town in weeks according to Max."

Dev generally went into the diner a couple of times a week, always the same days and time. It was where he and I had accidentally met a few months earlier.

"What about Junior? Has he seen Dev?" Junior Milliard ran the small, local grocery in *Deer Hollow*. Dev visited *Junior's Market* the first Monday of every month, arriving as the store opened at six o'clock in the morning so as to avoid running into anybody while he stocked up for the month.

"He showed up on schedule this month," Arno said, turning back to the cabin with a frown. "I don't like the looks of this, Joey."

Despair twisted painfully in my belly. I didn't like it either, but I'd been holding onto hope that it was all just a big misunderstanding. Arno's impressions all but ripped that hope away.

"It's still possible he hurt himself and he's at a hospital somewhere," Hal offered. He gave me a gentle look and I wanted to hug him. Clearly, he was trying to give me a lifeline. I just wasn't sure I could grasp it.

Arno nodded. "I'll check the hospitals within a thirty-mile radius."

Hal looked at me and lifted his brows. He wanted me to tell Arno about Cox. Frowning, I gave my head a small shake. I definitely wasn't ready to go there. So, I went someplace almost as bad. "Arno...is there any chance Devon's..."

"The body in the chipper?" He frowned. "I just don't know yet. But we'll grab some DNA samples from the cabin and of course the blood and compare it. That will tell us if it's a match."

"Are his fingerprints on file," Hal asked Arno.

"They are, but unfortunately the victim didn't have any to compare it to."

"No identifying marks at all?" Hal asked.

Sighing, Arno looked around to make sure we were alone before responding. "This was done by someone who knew what they were doing. The body was fed into the chipper arms first and then the head. Finger-prints, teeth and all facial features were obliterated. Most of the body was destroyed. From what was left, there was nothing. No surgery sites, no ink, nothing except some pretty serious nail fungus on one big toe."

I grimaced, trying to recall if Devon ever complained about nail fungus. I couldn't remember it if he had.

"Do you need us anymore?" Hal asked Arno.

"No. But if you have a card..."

Hal pulled out his wallet and extracted a business

card, handing it to Arno. "If you need me, I'll be staying at Joey's house."

Arno's eyebrows shot skyward.

Hal didn't bother to explain or justify his decision to stay with me. I liked that about him. As we walked away, I could feel Arno's gaze burning a trail over my back. I almost smiled.

CHAPTER EIGHT

*H*al waited until we'd gotten home and settled in with cold beers before he rocked my world.

Sitting on the other end of the couch I was curled up on, with a snoring pibl stretched out on her back between us, he looked me in the eye and just let fly.

"Tell me everything you know about Devon Little and his relationship to your parents."

I swallowed hard. I hadn't seen his question coming. He'd been so solicitous and gentle with me to that point, I guess I just figured he'd follow my lead and pretend there wasn't a giant pink elephant in the room.

I shook my head, opening my mouth to tell him it wasn't something I wanted to discuss.

He didn't even let me get the words out. "If you want my help on this, you need to be open with me about what's going on."

I frowned, anger rising as quickly as fear. Suddenly I found it hard to breathe. I shook my head again, pulling air into my lungs in a long, desperate inhalation. "Hal, I can't..."

"Yes. You can. I've only known you for a day but I already know that you're a strong woman, Joey. Much stronger than you give yourself credit for. I understand that you're in mourning. I get that. Believe me, I do. And if all of this..." he swung a hand towards the woods to indicate the murder and everything... "—wasn't happening right now you could indulge yourself in the luxury of continuing to mourn your parents. But I'm afraid something's happened to make that, not only inadvisable but dangerous." He leaned forward, his sexy gaze locked on mine and filled with intensity that made me swallow hard again. "I won't stay here and watch you drown in the intrigue swirling around you, Joey. If you won't let me help..."

He let the thought trail away, his handsome face taut with unhappiness. I didn't need to hear him speak the words. I understood what he was telling me. And as much as I hated it, he was right.

It was no longer possible to pretend everything I was experiencing was separate from my parents. It all seemed to be coming together under a single theme.

Something they'd done was coming back to bite me in the butt.

I sighed. "You're right. I'm sorry. Protecting myself from the memories has become a habit..." I thought about that for a moment, rolling the word around on my tongue. "Scratch that, it's become a lifeline. I'd always told myself that the things which were whispered about them were lies. I'd had to believe that or my life would have been turned inside out." I looked away, unwilling to see pity or disgust in his gaze. "I'm terrified I'll find out that they were nothing more than common criminals." And that knowledge would take me under...yanking every smidgeon of self-confidence I possess away.

"Things are rarely black and white, Joey. There's a good chance that we'll discover your parents were involved in something illegal. But that doesn't mean it was something horrible. Jaywalking is illegal. Speeding. Yet those are things we all do."

I dragged air into lungs that were tight and unco-operative. My chest hurt from the tears I wouldn't release. "And what if it *is* horrible? What do I do then?"

"You deal." His voice was hard, unbending, and my gaze shot to his. He held it, not wavering or giving me an inch of wiggle room.

"Easy for you to say," I told him. I didn't like the petulant tone in my voice but I couldn't seem to control it. It was either that or tears. And I couldn't give in to tears because the last time I had I hadn't surfaced from the gut-wrenching pain for weeks.

He shrugged. "Don't make the mistake of thinking you're the only one who's had pain, Joey."

He was right. I'd been wrapped up in my own

emotions for so long I'd stopped considering what other people were going through in their lives. In that moment I made myself a promise to find out what pain Hal had suffered. His expression was stern, his gaze unrelenting and his body had gone rigid.

He'd suffered a terrible loss of his own.

We sat in silence for several very long moments and then I started to talk. My voice was rusty with heartache at first, unshed tears clogged my throat, but as I trundled down that long-buried path of unexplored memories, it slowly became easier to find the words that made them real again.

"He's been my Uncle Dev for as long as I can remember. We have pictures of him holding me moments after I was born. Pictures of me riding on his shoulders at the zoo." I cleared my throat. "He was my father's closest friend and when I was born they made him my godparent."

Hal settled back against the cushions and fixed his intense, dark-green gaze on me, his expectant posture urging me onward.

"Dev worked with my father."

"Doing what?"

I shrugged. "The few times I came outside my teenage self to ask, he was vague. But he drove a truck so I assume he had something to do with acquiring items for the auction side of the business."

"Tell me about that."

I reached out and ran a hand over Caphy's velvet ears, smiling as she gave a dramatic groan and rolled belly up, all four stocky sticks poking straight up in the air. "I didn't know all that much about it, really. They brought a lot of farm equipment in and sold it on a consignment basis. They'd hold once-a-month auctions and people would come from all over the state."

"It must have been something to see."

I swung my gaze to his and found him smiling. I allowed myself to smile too. "Massive, actually. Acres and acres of...stuff. They were known for the quality of the equipment they sold."

"And lucrative," he added.

"Yes." I scanned a look around my home, seeing it as he must be seeing it. It wasn't hard to do because I'd felt like an intruder in the place ever since the will was read and it was awarded to me. "Dad bought only the best and he made sure he got top dollar for every item. Sellers from around the country came to him, wanting to auction off their goods through *Fulle-Proof Auctions*."

"I'm guessing he had to turn a lot of people down?"

My hand stilled on Caphy's belly and she whacked me with a paw to get it moving again. I would have grinned, but another memory had surfaced that ripped the smile right off my face. "He did."

"And was that ever a problem?"

"Not for my dad. He was unmovable once he'd made up his mind. But my mother used to go to him and beg him to help a friend. He rarely gave in to her."

And they'd had horrible fights about it. I shuddered under the memory.

"You told Cox the Feds had bothered your parents a lot over their last couple of years. What was that about?"

My fingers clenched around Caphy's heavy leg and I went very still. I wasn't sure I could talk about that. But I had no choice. So, I opened my mouth and forced the words through stiff lips. "They were accused of smuggling."

Hal blinked in surprise. "Smuggling? Of what, exactly?"

"My parents wouldn't talk to me about it so I don't really know. All I know is that they were really worried about something. And Uncle Dev disappeared for a few weeks. I never found out where he went."

Hal nodded. "I'm assuming the feds believed your parents were passing goods in the equipment they were auctioning off."

"Maybe." I shrugged. "It would have been easy to do. Which was why I've always wondered if it was true." My voice had dropped so low I barely heard the words myself. After a moment of silence fraught with tension, I forced myself to look up.

Hal was frowning, his gaze locked on Caphy's soft belly. He didn't speak for a long moment.

Finally, he sighed. "I hate to say it but we're going to have to talk to the feds."

"Oh no." I shoved upright on the couch, my knee bumping Caphy and making her yelp in surprise. She surged to her feet and stood looking around for an enemy. "I'm not giving that jerk what he wants. I'd rather die."

"That's exactly the point, Joey. You might die."

I snorted. "You're being overly dramatic."

"I don't think so. The murder on your property. Devon Little's disappearance. And now Cox showing up on your doorstep. These are not coincidences, Joey. Something's happening and I'm afraid you're right smack in the center of it. The only way to protect you is to know what we're up against. And, unfortunately, the feds are the only ones who can help us with that."

I set my jaw and shook my head. "No Cox. I'm not budging on that."

"Maybe we won't need him."

I skimmed him a narrow-eyed look. "I'm listening."

"I know someone..."

I waited but he didn't elaborate. "Someone?" I lifted my hands to indicate he should go on but it was his turn to look stubborn.

"I can't share a name with you until I get permission. But I might be able to get us what we need."

"Okay. I can live with that."

"In the meantime, you and I are glued together."

Before I could stop them, my lips curved up into a wide grin. "If you insist."

He shook his head, looking amused. "So, how about some dinner? We can talk about next steps while we eat."

"Um, I dial up a mean pizza."

He gave me a look. "I don't think so. My body's a temple."

I frowned. My body was really more of a pig wallow than a temple. I generally filled it with pretty much anything edible, and even some stuff that was suspect.

"Do you have food in the refrigerator?"

Hearing the "F" word, Caphy jumped off the couch and started bouncing around, barking with excitement.

"I think I might have some hummus. Maybe eggs. And, just FYI, never say the 'F' word around the dog."

He frowned. "I never say the 'F' word."

"Not *that* 'F' word," I explained as the cacophony increased to painful proportions. Caphy added running back and forth from the kitchen to the living room to her repertoire, her nails clicking a frantic tune on my hardwood floors. "We spell the 'F' word out here."

He grinned, moving past me and following a bouncing pibl toward the kitchen. "What? Miss Caphy doesn't spell?"

"Not yet," I murmured. "But give her time. If there's food involved she's highly motivated."

A mournful howl joined the litany of barking and dancing and I quickly realized my mistake. "Dangit! Now look what you made me do."

I followed his chuckle and my dog's noisy antics into the kitchen and headed right for the bin where I kept her food. There was no point trying to have adult conversation until the pitty was fed.

Kibble for the pibl was a priority.

CHAPTER NINE

I repositioned the cushions in the small of my back and settled more comfortably into the window seat. The massive oak tree huddling near the house reached for me, the limbs at the end of the tree's biggest branch looking like spindly fingers. I'd used the tree a hundred times growing up to sneak out of the house at night.

If my parents guessed what I was about they never said anything. I'd had my friends wait out of sight on our long drive and I'd hoofed it across the lawn to meet them there.

I smiled, realizing my childhood hadn't been filled only with bad memories. It would do me good to remember that as Hal and I plodded painfully through my past.

The grass beyond my window was painted in shapes created by a high, bright moon. The clouds that had skittered across the sky earlier, as Hal and I ate a delicious meal of hummus and fried egg wraps on the veranda, had skimmed away without bringing the rain they'd threatened.

A soft breeze, infused with the sweet scent of the roses reaching out to climb warm brick walls far below my perch, caressed my shoulders. Sighing softly, I rested my head against the window frame, letting the night wash over me.

A bullfrog belched its strange song alongside the pond. Crickets thrummed energetically. And, in the distance, an owl hooted a warning to its friends.

My eyes burned with weariness, but if I laid back down I'd just toss and turn. I'd tried to sleep. But Hal's careful questioning about my parents' lives and crimes had yanked big, hastily-applied stitches off the memories I'd tried to hide away.

I couldn't pretend anymore that the bad stuff hadn't happened.

I could no longer feign cluelessness.

Something had stepped into my world. Something ugly and feral. And my only hope of surviving it unscathed was to look it right in the eyes.

A soft thump had me turning to find my dog padding toward me. She'd been sound asleep when I'd climbed out of bed. Apparently, she'd finally realized I was gone. "Hey, pretty girl."

Caphy's tail dragged from side to side in lazy recognition of my greeting. She laid her squishy head on my lap and her tongue swept out to create a warm, wet patch on my boxers. "Am I interrupting your beauty sleep?"

She sighed dramatically and I chuckled. "Sorry, girl." I patted the cushion of the window seat and she bunched herself, launching effortlessly onto the seat. But rather than circling several times and coiling herself back into her favorite sleeping position, Caphy pressed her wide, wet nose against the screen and snuffled loudly.

"Lots of critters out there, huh, girl?"

Her tail twitched but she didn't look away. She dropped to her haunches and scanned a searching look over the yard. She was most likely scenting the big buck I'd seen gambol past only moments earlier. "You missed him, I'm afraid," I told her softly, reaching out to give her soft chin a scratch.

We sat in companionable silence for a long moment, both of us staring, transfixed, through the open window. A comfortable kind of calm crept over me. My eyes grew heavy, and I thought I might finally be able to sleep.

I was on the verge of dosing off, in fact, when I heard the low rumble of Caphy's growl. My eyes shot open. She hadn't moved. Her dense form was still framed by moonlight on the cushion near my feet, but she was vibrating with excitement.

I turned my gaze in the direction she was looking, thinking the buck must have returned. The grass around the pond was long and lush, like candy to the grazing animal population living around my house.

But the buck wasn't grazing by the pond.

Caphy's growl deepened, the sound thrumming through her body and vibrating against my foot. "What is it, girl?"

Her tail drifted sideways but it was only a half-hearted wag. Her startling green gaze was locked on the window, and the hair in front of her tail was standing on end.

I tugged the frilly curtain at the side of the window back and peered more carefully at the area beneath me. At first, I saw only shadows created by the trees and bushes.

But my instincts told me something lurked below. Maybe someone was looking at me that very moment. Someone trespassing in my life.

Something cold oozed through me at the thought, making gooseflesh pop on my arms and legs.

I eased back from the window, letting the curtain drop to give me cover as I kept my terrified gaze on the yard below.

The shadows danced as another breeze sifted past.

An owl screeched from a tree at the edge of the woods. I jumped at the sound. A painful tightness spread in my chest and I forced myself to breathe. I glanced toward the nightstand, my gaze searching out my phone.

If someone was there...

The shadows danced again and something disengaged from the base of the giant oak tree.

Caphy surged to her feet and her growl exploded into a warning bark. She lunged at the window, hitting the screen and nearly pulling it loose from the frame.

If she hit it again she would rip right through, falling to the ground below.

I shoved past a desire to run and get Hal, and instead wrenched free of the safe space behind the curtain and wrapped my arms around my dog, earning myself a painful scratch on the thigh as she tried to lunge at the window again.

The door in my room slammed open. "What is it?" Hal's deep voice called out.

It was all I could do to hold onto my dog and he wouldn't have heard my response anyway, over the din of her frantic barking.

The figure below stood for a moment, his face invisible in the shadows that clung to him, and then he slowly lifted an arm and pointed at me, before turning and taking off across the lawn.

Hal wrapped an arm around Caphy and dragged her backward, off the seat. "Close the window."

I did as he asked, my gaze finally turning to his. "Someone was down there. He was looking up at me." As I said the words my body was suddenly encased in ice. I shuddered at the memory of that featureless face focused in my direction.

"Where?" Hal demanded.

I pointed toward the woods. "He took off that way."

Hal spun on his heel and ran toward the door. "Stay here. Caphy, come!"

My dog didn't hesitate. She would have gone even without Hal's command. Unlike me, they were apparently both eager to face the intruder.

In that moment, I just wanted to climb back into bed and cover my head with blankets.

Like I'd done when I was a kid.

But I fought that instinct and forced myself to move. I couldn't let my dog and a near-stranger carry my water for me. Whatever was going on, I was starting to understand that it was most certainly something to do with my family.

It was my battle and, if I was half the man I always pretended to be, I needed to deal with it.

I followed the sound of Hal's footsteps through the house and then, after the crashing of the storm door, the throaty sound of Caphy's barking as she bounded across the yard.

There was a shout and my dog gave a high-pitched yelp, and I suddenly found myself plunging through the storm door, running across the porch and flying down the steps as I screamed her name.

Caphy's yelps had turned frantic, delivered in rapid-fire succession and getting softer as she apparently ran away. I searched the darkness for Hal's tell-tale form but didn't see him. I hoped he was dealing with whatever was hurting my dog.

Tears streamed down my face and panic flared. My feet thudded more quickly across the grass as fear extinguished any hesitation I might have nurtured to that point. The harsh rustle of dry needles stopped me in my tracks and I turned to see a long, low form shoot out of a large evergreen, not ten feet away from me.

The big coyote barely offered me a glance as it took off toward the pond and the woods beyond.

A coyote? My fear turned to panic as I recognized what Caphy's cries had meant. "Caphy?!" I shrieked into the night. "Hal?!"

Nothing.

I sucked in a deep breath and tensed, preparing to run, just as a hard hand clamped around my arm, and jerked me off my feet.

I stumbled backward, hitting a large form that smelled like smoke and garlic. A rock-hard arm snaked around my throat and tightened enough to make it difficult to breathe.

"Where is it?" a gruff voice demanded in my ear.

My fingers clawed at the heavy arm, feeling the coarse brush of hair against my skin. My nails dug into flesh and the taut band of the arm tightened around my throat. He dragged me off the ground and I felt my eyes bulging as I fought to breathe.

"Tell me or you'll die."

I tried to shake my head but it wouldn't move. My lips opened and the arm loosened slightly. "I don't..." the words caught in my throat and choked me.

"I know they told you where it is. If you tell me I'll let the dog live."

Tears slid hotly down my cheeks and I gave a little whimper. "I don't know what you want. I swear…"

The arm tightened around my throat and stars flashed in front of my eyes. I struggled against the impossible hold, feet kicking and hands digging into the unyielding flesh binding my throat. But nothing softened the hold. And I felt my limbs losing strength. The night grew even darker as my body started to fail me from the loss of air.

Something rumbled in the distance. My oxygen-starved brain tried to identify the sound but couldn't. And as I fell into the blackness, I felt my captor jerk, the heartbeats beneath my ear accelerating.

Suddenly the band of hard flesh was gone and I was falling, the ground coming up to smack me on the side of the head. I curled into the fetal position, coughing so hard I retched.

The distant grumbling had turned to snarls and the sharp click of snapping teeth. After the coughing I struggled to pull enough air into my lungs, my stomach roiling with the bright tang of nausea.

A husky voice called my name and something heavy and soft curled itself into my body. A warm, wet tongue swiped over my face and Caphy whimpered softly. My arms went around her, holding tight, even as she tensed beneath my arms.

"Joey!" Hal bent over me, his hands skimming hair from my face as I finally cranked my eyes open. Caphy licked the trail of tears from my face. Hal hit his knees on the grass beside me. "Are you hurt?"

I shook my head, struggling to push myself upright. "Just..." My voice was rusty. I cleared it and coughed again as Hal helped me sit. "My throat hurts."

He ran a fingertip over the tender area, frowning. "You'll have a bruise." His frown deepened. "He's lucky we didn't catch him."

Caphy barked once and burrowed into me. That was when I saw the glistening red on her shoulder. "She's hurt!"

Hal laid a hand on my dog's flank, nodding. "A little altercation with a coyote. I'm happy to report the coyote got the worst of it."

I buried my face in her throat, inhaling her sweet scent. "Thank god. I heard her yelping and saw the coyote. I was so afraid..."

Hal smiled. "Most of that yelping was from the coyote. Caphy will be okay. But we should take her to the vet and have it looked at. At the very least she'll need antibiotics."

I nodded, still holding her close. Then I remembered...

Lifting my head, I looked Hal in the eye. "Did you see him?"

"No. Caphy might have gotten a piece of him. But I called her back and he got away. I was too worried about you to follow."

I rubbed a hand over my throat. "He was choking me. I thought I was dead for sure."

Hal frowned again but said nothing.

Caphy shifted and yelped softly.

I pushed to my feet. "Come on, we need to take her in. We can talk about the other stuff later."

The nearest emergency veterinarian service was almost two hours away. Fortunately, one of the advantages of living in a small town where everybody had known everybody else for years was that vets and doctors still believed in going the extra mile for their clients.

So it was that, though Doc Beetle's voice was gruff with sleep when he answered his phone, he quickly woke enough to fire questions about Caphy's condition and then bark at me to bring her right into his clinic.

I was happy to comply.

CHAPTER TEN

$\mathscr{I}$t was entirely possible that Doc Beetle had been around when Moses went up the mountain. If he wasn't a contemporary of the great prophet, he'd at least been around when America became independent.

I was pretty sure he had callouses that were older than our constitution.

I tried the clinic door and found it locked. Peering through the small window in the door, I could only see a small section of the room near the front desk, where a night light provided enough illumination to move through the room and not much else.

"He isn't here yet," I told Hal.

Hal held Caphy against his chest, despite the fact that I told him she could walk just fine. I chewed the inside of my lip to keep from grinning as she stuck her tongue up his nostril for the tenth time, her tail whipping happily from side to side.

Hal was helpless to stop her from giving him a complete ear, nose and throat exam while he carried her from the car to the door. All he could do was turn his head when she assaulted him.

Then she just buried her tongue up to the root in his ear.

Hal shuddered at the wet invasion and glared at me when a laugh finally broke loose. "I told you she could walk."

A light flicked on inside the clinic and Hal skimmed me a long-suffering look. "I need a hashtag or something. After this I might even qualify for #metoo."

I grinned. "How about #againstmywoof."

"Very funny."

The door opened and I turned to find a tiny man with a face like a ten-year-old prune staring out at us. "Hey, Doc."

Doc Beetle, as everyone had called him for as long as I could remember, glowered up at Hal as if Caphy's injury and his having to get out of bed at midnight were all his fault. "You might as well bring her in."

I took a step back so Hal could move past me and got smacked in the face by Caphy's tail. "Ugh!"

Hal glanced over his shoulder. "Sorry."

"No worries," I murmured, rubbing my stinging cheek.

Doc ambled toward the exam rooms in the back. The speed with which he navigated the clinic belied his mummified appearance. His back was bent and his spindly legs were bowed, but clearly he still had a lot of rev in his gnarled old engine. "Put her on the table."

Doc opened a cabinet and pulled out a small glass bottle, a syringe, some cotton pads and a squirt bottle of rubbing alcohol. He set everything on the counter near the table and washed his hands, taking his time and using lots of soap.

Hal settled my dog onto the table and scooted over to make room for me near her head. I bent to kiss her squishy head and her tongue immediately snapped out and found my nostril, doing her roto rooter shtick.

I jerked away from her attack. "No thanks, sweet girl," I told her. "I don't need a nostril exam right now."

Doc Beetle fixed small, brown eyes on me, the caterpillars perched above them wiggling as he pursed wrinkly lips. "Your throat is bruised."

I shrugged. "It's nothing. I'm more worried about Caphy."

He grunted softly. "Tell me about her," he demanded in his wobbly voice.

"She has a bite mark on her shoulder which seems really painful," I told him. "We figured she'd probably need antibiotics." I petted my dog's thick paw and fidgeted, made uneasy by the vet's surly attitude. He spoke little and, unless he was talking to one of his patients, he rarely wore any expression happier than disgust so I always felt as if he were judging me and I was failing.

I bit my bottom lip as he bent over Caphy and began to probe the wound with his twisted fingers.

My dog's head snapped around and her tongue came out, frantically licking his hand. Doc Beetle smoothed his hand over Caphy's snout. "It's all right, girl. You'll be okay."

I relaxed slightly. Though I'd told myself and Hal that she was okay, I'd been nursing a niggling worry that the damage was worse than it appeared.

Doc Beetle ran his hands over her entire body, searching for other damage, and then grabbed the alcohol and squeezed a good measure of it over the wound. He used the cotton to wipe and stretch the wound to get a better look at it. He clucked his tongue and I stiffened.

Tongue clucking was Doc's way of signaling trouble.

"What is it?" I asked, my pulse spiking with alarm.

He barely glanced up at me and, when he did, the beady brown gaze was filled with kindness.

Kindness! I clutched the edge of the stainless-steel exam table. Caphy was going to die. "Just tell me the worst. I can handle it."

Doc's gaze narrowed and the quick warmth fled them, leaving behind the disgust I was more used to.

He shook his head and reached for a long, stainless steel pair of grippers that was laid out with several other tools on a pristine white towel on the counter. He inserted the tool carefully into the wound and I clutched Caphy's leg more tightly, alarmed that he hadn't sedated her or anything.

She licked my hand as if comforting me.

After a moment, Doc nodded his head and retracted the tool, holding it up for us to see. A curved, deadly-looking tooth was clutched between the gripper's jaws.

"Is that a coyote tooth?" Hal asked, leaning closer to examine it with interest.

"It is." Doc stepped on the trash can pedal and dropped the tooth inside. He filled one of the syringes from the contents of the bottle and injected it in Caphy's hip. "This wound is deep. I might need to put a drain in it."

"If that's what she needs," I said dejectedly.

His glower deepened. "You sound like I'm threatening to snip off one of your fingers, young lady."

I winced. "It's just, I hate those things. They're so messy."

He eyed the wound again. "I want this wound kept open for a while so it can drain. You up to scrubbing it a couple of times a day to make sure it stays this way?"

I nodded enthusiastically. "Absolutely."

He shook his head again. "All right. We'll try it your way for a couple of days. But don't let it close up. I gave her antibiotics and I'll send you home with some pills too. Coyote bites can be nasty things. We don't want to mess around."

"Thanks, Doc."

He stood there for a minute, smoothing his hand over my dog's soft coat and almost smiling. He looked totally at peace when working with one of his patients. Though he'd been a vet for decades, he still clearly loved what he did. I envied him that contentment.

He suddenly lifted his gaze as if sensing me staring at him. "I heard what happened out at your place."

I blinked at the sudden change of subject. Then nodded. "It was pretty terrible."

"I can imagine." He twisted his lips, the movement deepening the billions of wrinkles on his small face. "Thing is, I remember some of the stuff your folks went through."

Hal straightened, clearly interested. "Do you think there's a connection?"

Doc glanced at Hal, his expression unfriendly. "Who are you?"

I had a face/palm moment. "I'm so sorry. Doc this is Hal Amity. He's here to help me figure out if that body in my woods has something to do with me."

"Why on earth would it?"

"I thought you were implying..." Hal started.

Doc waved a hand in the air dismissively. "I didn't say anything of the kind. I just..." He shook his head again. "I'm just hoping the Feds aren't going to start harassing you now too."

A light bulb went on. "You saw Cox in town, didn't you?"

Doc expelled air. He moved to the cabinet and pulled down a large bottle of pills, dumping some into his hand and counting them out. He dropped several into a small bottle and twisted the cap, handing it to me. "He came here."

"Why?" Hal asked, seemingly undaunted by Doc's cold demeanor toward him.

Doc seemed to be ignoring Hal for a long moment, but then he looked up, capturing Hal's gaze. "Brent and Joline Fulle were good people," he told Hal almost angrily.

"Doc..." I said, intending to tell him he didn't need to defend them to us.

He shook his head. "No, Joey, this needs sayin'. The feds tortured your poor folks. They didn't deserve it. And you'll never convince me they didn't have a hand in that plane crash."

I gasped, stars bursting before my eyes as shock sliced through me. "What? Are you serious?"

"As a heart attack. The government doesn't like it when citizens play them for fools. Your folks, well, they maximized their business, if you know what I mean. They might have bent some rules but they didn't hurt anybody. But Cox is obsessed with them. He's determined to prove they did something illegal."

"Did they?" Hal asked quietly.

To my vast surprise, Doc seemed to be considering Hal's question. He finally shook his head. "I don't believe they did, son. But it's going to be up to you to find out. Cox isn't trying to clear their names. If he has his way they'll be painted as criminals." He glanced at me. "And he'll take you down too, Joey if you don't give him what he wants."

"But what is that?" I asked, thinking about the gruff demand in my ear as I'd struggled to survive a mere hour earlier. *Where is it?* my attacker had asked. I wouldn't be able to give him or Cox what they wanted. I didn't even know what *it* was.

"Only Cox knows, young lady. But keep your guard up with him. Don't be fooled into thinking he's trying to help. I'm afraid helping you is the last thing on Cox's beady little brain."

CHAPTER ELEVEN

*B*y the time we got home again it was nearly three AM. I was so tired I fell into bed and, Caphy stretched out beside me, already snoring, I dropped into a deep, dreamless sleep.

The sun was bright through my window when I awoke several hours later. I stretched and yawned, reaching out to pet my dog awake.

My hand fell on the cool, empty sheet and my eyes shot open. That was when my nose registered the delicious scent of something sweet and yeasty.

I shoved back the covers and tugged boxers on with my tee-shirt. I found Hal in the kitchen, wearing hot pad gloves and settling a cookie sheet onto the stovetop.

Caphy was sitting as close to him as she could, her gaze locked like a laser on the freshly baked cinnamon rolls filling the sheet.

Hal looked up as I entered the kitchen. "Morning." He smiled and reached for a small bowl on the counter. "Coffee's made. Help yourself."

I walked over and eyed the rolls, my mouth watering as he drizzled glaze from the bowl over them, using a large spoon. "Lizard sneakers."

He frowned. "Huh?"

I pointed to the pan. "That, right there. That's cooler than lizard sneakers."

He narrowed his gaze at me and I shook my head. "It's just something my mom used to say. Those look delicious. Did you unroll them from a cardboard tube?"

He gave me a look filled with horror. "Amitys don't unroll their food. These are made from scratch."

I shrugged. "I didn't realize I had the *scratch* needed to make something that exotic and wonderful." I reached for one and got my hand lightly smacked for my trouble. "Hey!"

"Coffee. Sit." He pointed to the table and I glared at him. Fortunately, a drop of icing had landed on my hand when he smacked it. I licked it up as I headed for the coffee pot, nearly swooning as buttery sweetness coated my tongue.

As soon as I was seated with my coffee, Hal carried a plate of freshly glazed rolls over and set them on the table in front of some small plates. There were two bowls of fresh fruit beside the plates. "I *know* I didn't have this in my fridge," I told him.

"That fruit is courtesy of the produce stand up the road. Caphy and I visited it this morning."

I plucked a fat, red strawberry from the bowl and took a bite, squirting sweet juice over myself in the process.

Hal handed me a napkin.

Caphy smacked her lips and I looked down to where she sat, her fat, squishy head on his lap and her pretty green gaze riveted on Hal's every move.

My dog had deserted me for a guy with food.

Dang that sucked. In a petty and desperate move, I plucked another berry from my bowl and held it up so she could see it. "Come here, Caphy girl."

She jumped up and ran around Hal to get to me. "Sit," I instructed. She plopped her wide behind down and carefully took the strawberry from between my fingers. Her tail thumped Hal's chair.

"Here girl," he said, a gleam in his eye. He held a hunk of gooey cinnamon roll between his fingers. Caphy whipped around and barked with excitement when she saw it. "Sit."

Her butt hit the ground so hard she made an "umph" sound from the impact. Hal gave her the pastry and grinned at me.

"You don't want to get between a girl and her dog, buddy."

He chuckled. "Just teasing. I know better. Besides, this dog loves you to distraction. She wouldn't have left your side this morning if I hadn't bribed her with a dog cookie."

I flushed with pleasure. "Well, it's good to know that when she dumps me it'll be for something important like food."

He nodded as if I'd made a serious observation. "Eat up. We have a lot of work to do today."

I grabbed a roll and bit into it, moaning softly as the tender pastry melted on my tongue. As soon as I'd swallowed I asked, "What's on the agenda?"

He chewed and swallowed, chasing the bite of roll with a sip of coffee before answering me. "We need to talk to your friend the cop about an ID on that DNA he pulled from the cabin. Then I need to talk to my friend at the FBI about Cox."

"Will they be straight with you?"

"I think so. I've heard of Cox before. He's not well-liked."

"I guess even in the government being cray-cray is frowned upon."

"Yeah."

I ate some melon that tasted like it had just been picked, licking my lips as I swallowed. "Good."

"It is good. Haven't you ever been to that stand? It's not more than a quarter-mile up the road."

I shook my head, then hesitated. "Wait, which way up the road?"

"Where *Goat's Hollow* meets *CR57*. Why?"

"What time did you stop in?"

"Around six AM. What are you thinking?"

"I haven't bought anything at that stand, but now that you brought it up I know exactly where it is. It's not far from Devon's driveway or the spot where the chipper entered my woods."

"You're thinking the people who run the stand might have seen something?"

I shrugged. "It's worth asking."

"You're right. It's definitely worth that."

Grabbing what was left of my roll, I stood up. "Just give me fifteen minutes to tend to Caphy's wound and get dressed."

∾

*H*al pulled into the small gravel lot where the stand was located. The space was actually an overlook, at the edge of a vista filled with trees and the wide, sparkling ribbon of a river in the distance. It was on the opposite side of the road from my place and overlooked a largely unused portion of the *Deer County State Park*, a thousand-acre extravaganza of trees, rocky ridges, rough-hewn pathways and the before mentioned, *Fawn River*.

I stood at the guard rail and looked out over the park, thinking about the times I'd hiked it with my parents before their deaths. I needed to hit the trails again. Caphy would love it. The park was filled with wildlife for her to scent and chase. And she loved to play in the cool waters of the *Fawn*.

Then I spotted the Coyote dens dotting the side of the nearest ridge and all thoughts of taking my dog into the park fled.

"Joey?" I turned with a start and found Hal watching me curiously. "Sorry. I was just remembering when I used to hike through this park."

He nodded. "It's beautiful."

"It is. But then there's that..." I pointed toward the dens and he narrowed his gaze, clearly trying to figure out what he was looking at. I'd forgotten he was a city boy. "Coyote dens."

"Ah. Well, maybe not then."

"Hey, Caphy!"

I turned at the sound of the pleasant voice and smiled. Edith Pickering had been my second-grade teacher back in the day. I hadn't realized she was working at the stand. I said as much to her as Caphy and I walked her way and she grinned. "It's worse than that, honey. I own this stand." She glanced at Hal.

I vaguely remembered that she and her husband had a large parcel of farmland about ten miles outside of *Deer Hollow*. They'd been good customers of my dad's auction.

I accepted a hug and Caphy was instructed to sit and give Edith her paw before she received a handful of plump, sweet blueberries. "The last time I saw this sweet girl she was small enough to fit into a shoebox." Edith scratched my dog under the chin, earning herself a squinty-eyed look of pleasure from the pibl.

I laughed. "I doubt she could fit her head into a shoebox now."

Edith cupped the aforementioned head between

her hands and grinned at my dog. Caphy grinned back, her wide, pink tongue lolling out the side of her mouth. "She's adorable." Then she spotted the wound on Caphy's shoulder and winced. "Coyote?"

"Yeah. How'd you know?"

"Our Bear was bitten a few times. Nasty creatures. But I understand they're just trying to survive." Shaking her head, she stood with a groan. "Don't let anybody ever tell you it's easy to get old, honey. Basically, it sucks."

"Beats the alternative," I told her with a grin.

"Says a child of not even thirty," she responded with a sparkle in her brown eye. "What happened there, Joey?" She pointed to her own throat and I flushed. I'd tried to cover the bruising with makeup but apparently I hadn't done a good enough job.

"Oh, well, you know how clumsy I am. I tripped over Caphy and..." I shrugged, leaving the rest to her imagination.

She patted my arm and glanced at Hal again, clearly looking for an introduction.

"Edith, this is Hal Amity. He's visiting from Indy."

"Indy, huh? What brings you down this way, Hal Amity?" She scanned an assessing look over him, no doubt trying to figure out if we were sleeping together yet.

Despite the fact that city folks tended to believe country folk were backward and shy about sex, it just wasn't the truth. Country dwellers grew up watching special animal activities in the barnyard and discussing which livestock should be bred with which so that we actually had a very down-to-earth view of the act itself. Religious scruples aside.

In my case, I happened to know that, at the last town fair there'd been an underground pool over when I was finally going to get a boyfriend. I didn't know how far out the pool had gone, but I was pretty sure the weakest among the contestants had already been punted to the curb. Knowing Edith, she was probably still in the running.

"He's here to help me figure out why somebody was murdered on my land."

Edith thought about that for a moment and then sighed. "I'm sure it had nothing to do with them, honey."

She meant my parents. I shrugged. "I'll feel better when I know that for sure."

She nodded. "Now what can I sell you? I have some really delicious sweet corn from Florida."

Hal frowned. "Florida? Why not local."

"Oh, we haven't picked ours yet. It will be a few months yet."

I nodded. "I'll take six ears please." I glanced at Hal as Edith was bagging up the corn for me. He inclined his head to let me know I should take the lead. "And speaking of what happened in my woods..."

Edith clucked her tongue. "The body in the chipper." She handed me the bag of corn. "Sounds like the title of a murder mystery doesn't it?"

I nodded. "When Hal told me he was here this morning..."

Edith turned a surprised look on my PI. "You were here? What time?"

"Around six. There was a young girl here at the time."

Edith nodded. "My granddaughter. She goes into work at nine so she fills in early mornings for me."

He nodded. "I see the resemblance."

"I'll take that as a compliment," Edith said, beaming.

I'd seen Lori Pickering and Edith should definitely take it as a compliment. The girl was gorgeous. "I didn't realize she was still here in *Deer Hollow*. I figured she'd have moved to Indianapolis by now."

"Or Chicago," Edith said, nodding. "She'd planned on going to Northwestern when she graduated last fall, but then her mom got sick and she just kind of gave up on that idea."

"Lilly's sick? I'm so sorry to hear that." In that moment I understood how far I'd let myself grow away from my community after my parents died. I needed to fix that. I'd always cherished the people in *Deer Hollow* and, unlike Lori Pickering, I had no desire to move away from them.

Even emotionally. "Please let me know if I can help."

Edith patted my hand. "Thanks, honey."

"How early does the stand open in the mornings," Hal asked.

"Five thirty or six. Whenever we can make it out here and get it stocked up. We try to catch the people traveling to the bigger towns for work." She frowned. "Why do you ask?"

"We were wondering if maybe you'd seen someone loading or unloading an ATV the other morning."

"The day we found the body," I added helpfully.

Edith paled. "Oh my, was that around here?"

I pointed into the woods. "Not far at all. We think they went into the woods about an eighth of a mile down the road."

She stared in the direction I pointed and clucked her tongue. "Dang rascals. I just can't believe it...in our lazy little town."

"So, you didn't see anything?"

"No. But like I said, Lori would have probably been here then."

"Have you seen anybody pulling a chipper around?" Hal asked.

"No. Sorry. Except for Buck, of course."

Hal skimmed me a look before returning his attention to Edith. "Buck Mitzner?"

Her mouth tightened in the usual reaction to hearing Buck's name. "He's always pulling those things around. They rent them out, you know."

"We did know that," I told her. "When you saw him was he hauling it toward *Mitzner's* or away?"

She pointed south of *Deer Hollow*. "He was going that way, toward his place."

CHAPTER TWELVE

*B*uck Mitzner was in the back lot, showing some mature trees to a couple who I thought might have just moved into the new subdivision on the edge of town. Ever since the developer bought the huge tract of farmland and started building on it, my peaceful little town had begun to change. Some of the changes, like new stores and restaurants springing up in *Deer Hollow* and the surrounding countryside, were welcome. But having a bunch of strangers move into town was disconcerting. And I was having trouble adjusting to it.

"Joey!!!"

The high-pitched voice came from behind me and I spun, a grin already finding my face as I recognized the tall, auburn-haired beauty hurrying my way. She held out her arms as she all but ran my way, only the spindly heels of her unsuitable shoes keeping her from an all-out run.

I opened my own arms and accepted the hug she offered. "Lis! I didn't know you were in town," I told my best friend from grade school on. "Why didn't you call?"

Lis Villa shook her head, giving me her trademark, "don't be stupid" look. "I've been calling. You never answer your phone."

I flushed with embarrassment. "That's not possible. I know your number. I would have answered."

"Except I have a new number now, Jo Jo." She expelled a disgusted breath. "Why are you screening your calls anyway?"

I skimmed Hal a quick look, unwilling to talk about the harassment I'd suffered after my parents died. Instead, I shook my head. "I have my reasons." I hugged her again, so happy to see her. "It's been way too long. Are you here to stay for a while?"

Lis, short for Melissa, because...Melissa Villa... gave me a pout. "Unfortunately, not. I'm only here a couple of nights. I have a shoot in Guadalajara on Friday."

"Guadalajara?" I gave her a fake grimace. "That's really too bad. You must hate it."

She laughed and ruffled my hair like she'd done since we were in first grade together. It had annoyed the heck out of me then and it hadn't gotten any easier to take over the years. I smoothed a hand over my messy red-blonde locks. Lis gave my PI a meaningful glance and he offered his hand, the interest on his face obvious. "Hal Amity. I'm helping Joey with a...personal matter."

There was no missing the answering interest in my old friend's perfect face. "Personal, huh?"

Hal flushed slightly. To my vast surprise, annoyance surged as the two clasped hands, their perfect bodies bending toward each other in a seemingly subconscious way. "This is my *oldest* and dearest friend," I told Hal. I promise, my emphasis on the word "oldest" was unintentional. But it was heartfelt. "We've known each other since grade school."

Lis narrowed her dark blue eyes at me. "I'm only four months older than you, Joey. You need to get over it." Hal and Lis grinned at each other, their gazes locked on and zeroed out.

I'd been forgotten.

I squelched a sigh. It wasn't as if I wasn't used to being overshadowed by my best friend. She was absolutely gorgeous. And she was one of the nicest people I knew too. She basically had everything. Especially now. Since she'd become one of the world's most famous fashion models.

"So..." I squeaked out, clearing my throat to remove the traitorous frog. "What brings you to *Deer Hollow?*"

For a moment I didn't think she was going to drag her gaze from Hal. But she finally skimmed a look my way, grimacing. "I have an appointment with Heather Masterson."

"The artist?" Hal looked suitably impressed. "She lives here?"

"She does," I told him. "Remember when we were discussing the fact that *Deer Hollow* is home to several artists?"

He barely glanced my way before returning his full attention to Lis. "I saw her work in a gallery in Indy. It's impressive."

I crossed my arms crankily over my chest, which wasn't nearly as big or firm as Lis', "If you like strangely dressed people with big feet." I shrugged. "I guess."

I was actually overstating the issue. Heather Masterson had hit it big not all that long ago because her portraits were so unique. She painted people into nature, wearing twigs and stuff, and she always over-emphasized their feet and hands. For whatever reason.

I'd never actually met the woman. But I'd heard she was very strange.

Lis threw me a grin. "I hate that I have to do this. I think her portraits are ugly. But my agent is insist-ing." She sighed and then brightened. "Hey! You want to come with me?"

"Oh. I don't know."

"Come on, Jo Jo. It'll be fun."

"You should go," Hal said.

"But...Is it safe?"

Before he could respond, Lis laughed. "I doubt she'll stab you with a paintbrush while we're there."

Heat flared in my cheeks. I didn't want to tell my friend about the body in the wood chipper or the attack from the night before. I hadn't seen her in years and I didn't want to spend the time together talking about terrible things. So, I forced a laugh and nodded. "I'd love to come. When are you going up there?"

"Eight o'clock in the morning?" She lifted a perfectly sculpted eyebrow and I knew she was remembering the old, spoiled me who'd slept until nearly ten o'clock every morning.

"Great. I'll be ready."

"We'll pick you up," Hal interjected and I blinked, looking at him in surprise. "You don't mind if I come, do you? I'd love to meet Ms. Masterson."

Lis squealed and gabbled on for minutes on end about how much she didn't mind. Until I wanted to hork all over her shoes.

Hal couldn't stop smiling.

And me? I was less enthusiastic at the idea of my PI spending the day drooling over my best friend. But hey, who was I to squash a budding romance?

Lis left us a few minutes later, after Hal loaded a flowering bush into the back of her car. For her mother, she explained happily. Mrs. Villa would love it.

Waving as she drove out of the lot, I started toward the main building, leaving Hal to catch up. He reached for the door as we arrived and I shoved past, yanking it open myself. I could almost feel his confusion at my cold, angry mood but I was the last person who could explain it to him.

I had no idea myself why I was so mad.

Fortunately, Buck Mitzner was behind the counter when I walked into the cool dimness of the store. I squared my shoulders and headed right for him, glad to have somebody to beat up on. "Mr. Mitzner," I said in a firm, hostile tone. "I have some more questions for you."

He looked up and blinked in surprise, looking past me as Hal approached. "You two again? Why are you harassing me?"

Before Hal could respond I launched a direct hit. "Maybe if you hadn't lied to us we wouldn't have to bother you again."

Buck's face turned an unattractive shade of red. "I don't think you meant to call me a liar, Joey Fulle."

"I think I did. When we asked you about the chipper you pretended it had been stolen. Why didn't you tell us it was at your house?"

Buck's chins wobbled as outrage overtook him. He lifted a hand and stabbed a finger at me, mere inches from my chest. "You'd better learn some manners, girl."

I slapped the hand away and Buck's face flashed purple before he pulled himself upright and started around the counter.

Hal moved smoothly between us. "Mr. Mitzner. What Joey means to say is that we have an eye-witness who saw you pulling the chipper out of town the night before it was found on Joey's property. Can you tell us where you were taking it?"

Buck stared at me for a long moment, his chest heaving with rage. Then, to my surprise, he looked away and pulled in a long breath. He walked back around the counter and picked up a pile of receipts. "I have nothing to say to you. Get out of my store."

"Okay. No problem, Mr. Mitzner."

I gave Hal wide eyes and opened my mouth to argue, but his next statement made me snap it shut again. "I guess we'll just go to the police with our new information then. Have a nice day." He wrapped a hand around my arm and tugged me gently toward the door. We were outside, standing in the pleasant shade of the porch roof when Mitzner came through the door.

Hal kept a restraining hand on me as we started toward his car in the lot.

"Hold on," Buck growled.

Hal kept walking.

Mitzner swore and I smiled. "I said hold on!"

Hal took a couple more steps before stopping and I thought Mitzner was going to explode. Even with my back to him, I could feel the vibrations in the force.

We turned slowly and Hal gave him a serene smile. "Was there something you wanted to tell us, Mr. Mitzner?"

Mitzner's hands were folded into fists at his side and he fairly vibrated with rage. But I felt no pity for him. He was a jerk. And things could have gone very differently if he hadn't been so nasty to us.

I conveniently squashed the knowledge that I probably hadn't helped his attitude by charging at him like a bull.

"It was at my house."

For a beat I was confused. Then I caught up and sucked air. Was Buck admitting to chipping the body in my woods?

Hal frowned. "The chipper was at your house?"

"That's what I said."

Buck's face was purple with rage. I vaguely wondered if he was going to stroke out on us.

"How did it get into my woods?" I asked him.

Buck seemed to deflate a little. Some of the angry color left his face and when he spoke, it was with an almost pleading quality. "I don't know how it got there. You have to believe me. I brought the chipper home to clear some of the woods around my house so I could build a patio. When I went to bed it was sitting at the side of my house. And when I got up in the morning it was gone. The next thing I knew it was being reported as a murder weapon." He shook his head, his hands flexing and unflexing at his sides. "I swear to you I had nothing to do with killing that guy."

"Guy? Do you know who it was?" Hal asked.

Mitzner's color flared again and his jaw tightened with belligerence. "I just told you I had nothing to do with the murder."

"But you said 'that guy' as if you knew who it was," Hal pointed out very reasonably. "It could just as easily have been a woman."

Except that it probably couldn't have been, I mused. The coroner, a.k.a. Rashton Blessed at *Blessed Rest Funeral Home*, might not know who was killed, but he surely could tell by the size of the bones if it was a man or a woman. But I kept my mouth shut because Hal was being smart. It seemed as if Buck was telling us the truth, but we didn't know for sure. He could just be very good at lying.

"I have no idea who was in that chipper," Buck growled out. "And if I did I'd tell Arno, not you." He nodded as if making a sudden decision. "I don't know you, son. But I do know that you're an outsider. You have no business sticking your nose into this thing." He half-turned and then stopped. "Tell the cops or not. I don't really care. Arno isn't going to like you sticking your nose into his investigation. It's more likely that you'll get in trouble instead of me."

~

"We have just enough time to talk to Lori Pickering before lunch," I told Hal.

He frowned briefly, his foot easing down on the brake as he made the turn into *Deer Hollow*. "Ah, the produce stand girl." He nodded. "Okay. Where does she work?"

"*Brats versus Broads*," I told him.

He gave me a blank look. "Huh?"

"It's a daycare center at the other end of Main Street. Just keep going straight."

He shook his head but didn't comment on the name. Personally, I loved it. Politically correct we were not in *Deer Hollow*. It was one of the things I liked best about the place.

"How do you survive without cameras and lights all over the place?" Hal asked as we drove through the town's only traffic light.

"In happiness and tranquility. Besides," I told him with a grin. "I don't have to worry about how I look all the time. Imagine if I had to fret over a picture of me in baggy sweats, ancient black sneakers and no makeup, being sent off for all of the Sheriff's Deputies to chuckle over."

He gave me a speculative look. "You'd actually go out of the house like that?"

"Yep. Hair sticking up like a porcupine's girl-friend. I do it all the time " I bit the inside of my lip to keep from smiling at the look of `horror on his face.

Fortunately, he was saved from responding as we pulled up on the stone ranch that housed *Brats versus Broads*. He stopped the SUV at the curb, directly in front of a massive sign that showed a cartoonish female character with long dark hair, wearing superhero garb and wielding a whip. Facing off with the "Broad" was a masked baby in a diaper bearing the stars and stripes and pointing a bottle that shot lightning bolts at his nemesis.

I chuckled like I always did when I saw the sign.

"Well, I'll be..." Hal murmured. "You weren't kidding."

I snorted out a laugh. "Come on, let's get this interview over with. I'm starving."

CHAPTER THIRTEEN

*T*rue to the fun-loving theme of the daycare center, the interior was thick with giant stuffed animals and all possible manner of toys. Large posters of superheroes covered much of the open wall space and the floor was dotted with blocks, books, and an impressive array of toys. Seated among the toys were about a dozen kids of various sizes and ages. I judged the oldest to be around five and the youngest was an infant.

Lori Pickering was holding said infant and feeding it a bottle. She looked up when we came inside and scanned a look over Hal. The way her eyes lit up at the sight of him, I figured she either remembered him from that morning, or was giving definite consideration to making him her baby daddy.

I waved and threw her a smile that felt a bit tight. I was starting to wonder how Hal got anything done with women practically throwing themselves at him all the time.

An unexpected shriek sent both Hal and me straight into the air, just as the world's tiniest super villain leaped into view. The dark-haired desperado gave us one, hostile glance and then took advantage of our discombobulated state, shoving his plastic gun into the spot on Hal's body nearest his line of sight.

Hal jumped back with a short bark of pain and I pressed my lips together to restrain a grin.

"Stick 'em up, mister!" the kid demanded.

I just had time for the irreverent thought that my poor embattled PI might not be sticking anything up for a while, when Lori suddenly appeared at my elbow. "Billy Rogers! What did I tell you about assaulting people with your pistol?"

I had a feeling that sentiment would be a recurring theme in Billy Rogers' future.

The little boy, who looked to be about three years old, twisted his cute but clearly evil face into a belligerent scowl. "You're not the boss of me."

"Actually," Lori told him with a quick glance at Hal. "I *am* the boss of you. Now you apologize to this nice man right now."

Belligerent Billy crossed short, fat arms over his chest and stuck out his bottom lip, clearly refusing to buckle to "the man".

Or, in this case, "the *wo*man".

"Do you want to go into time out?"

Personally, I thought that was a stupid question. Nobody *wanted* to go into time out. Did they?

Scanning a look over Hal, whose handsome face was greener than usual and a bit pinched looking, I adjusted my thinking. I was pretty sure he'd enjoy time out if there were no assault pistol attack toddlers there.

"Uh uh," Billy admitted, no less belligerent than before the threat.

"Then apologize right now."

Billy continued to glare at her a moment longer before giving in. "Thorry."

Hal looked at him as if he were a particularly nasty type of bug.

"Now go and play nicely. We're going to have lunch soon."

That happy thought sent Billy haring loudly around the room, threatening everyone with his plastic weapon.

Lori gave Hal's offended area a sympathetic look. "I'm so sorry. Are you okay?"

Hal cleared his throat and I got the distinct impression he was afraid to speak for fear his voice would be all high and squeaky.

"Do you need a band-aid or something?" I asked, with saccharine sweetness.

He glared in my direction. Then he very pointedly dismissed me, focusing on Lori Pickering. "I don't know if you remember me..."

"I do!" she nearly screamed. The baby in her arms

jerked under the unexpected heft of her exclamation and gave a short cry before latching hungrily back onto the bottle.

She flushed slightly. "You came by the produce stand earlier."

Hal nodded. "I don't think I introduced myself. I'm Hal Amity." He offered her his hand and she shifted the infant so she could shake it. "Lori Pickering. It's a pleasure to meet you."

Judging by the way she was undressing him with her eyes, I could only presume that was a vast understatement. I suddenly found myself very motivated to drag her gaze away from Hal. "We need to ask you some questions about the other night," I said in my most official tone of voice.

Lori looked at me, blinking rapidly. "What other night?"

"The other night when a dead guy ended up in my woods."

Someone sucked air behind me and I jerked around to find a small girl with long, blonde curls looking up at me through eyes that reminded me of those big-eyed cartoon creatures.

I'd always found those to be a little creepy.

The little girl clutched an upside-down rag doll in one pudgy hand and nibbled on her perfect, pink rosebud lips. "Thomebody died?" she asked while imploring me with tear-filled eyes. "My doggie died. It made me thad." She sniffed loudly and I turned to Lori, totally out of my element.

Lori glared at me before crouching down beside the little girl and murmuring soothing nonsense to her.

I glanced at Hal and found him giving me judgy eyebrows.

"What?" I asked in a harsh whisper. "I didn't know she was skulking around back there."

He shook his head. "Inside voice, Joey." That was when I saw the humor sparking in his sexy green gaze.

I gave him a twisted grin.

"Let's keep our voices down, shall we?" Lori said to no one in particular. Even though everyone there knew exactly *who* she was talking to.

I fought the sigh trembling on my lips. It had been a while since I'd been reduced to feeling like a naughty child. "Thorry...I mean, sorry. You heard about the chipper thing in my woods?"

Lori nodded. "Everyone has."

Her statement wasn't the generalization it appeared to be. If I knew *Deer Hollow*...and I did...the murder would be a regular topic in every home within a fifty-mile radius.

"We think the chipper was pulled into the woods with an ATV vehicle. Do you remember seeing or hearing anything early that morning?"

Lori shook her head. "I actually got to the stand about a half-hour late that day. I overslept." She flushed prettily. "I'm sure your guy was long gone by then." She shuddered. "But I'm not happy to hear how close I was to the site and the..." She glanced quickly around to make sure there were no more pint-sized eavesdroppers. "...body."

"You didn't pass a vehicle with an ATV on your way to the stand?" Hal asked.

"No. Sorry."

"Did you hear anything? Engine sounds in the woods or up the road a bit?" I asked.

She barely looked at me. "Nothing like an ATV, no. I wish I could be more help."

Hal produced a business card and handed it to her. "If you think of anything..."

Nodding, she took the card, her fingers skimming his. Then she frowned. "Hold on. I didn't see or hear anything that morning, but there was someone who might have."

"Who's that?" I asked a little too eagerly.

"Heather Masterson was there. She was up on the ridge when I arrived, sketching the sunrise."

"Did it look like she'd been there a while?" Hal asked.

"It did, actually. She'd spread a blanket or something on the ground and there was a thermos of coffee next to her chair."

"Thank you," Hal said, reaching to grip her hand again. "You've been very helpful."

I thrust my hand in her direction. "Yeah. Thanks, Lori. We actually have an appointment with Heather in the morning. We'll ask her about it."

Lori dropped Hal's hand but didn't take mine, only nodding with an assessing look in her hazel eyes.

A door opened at the back of the room and an older woman with graying brown hair stuck her head through. "Lunchtime!" There was a red strap around the woman's neck, tied in an oversized bow. When she moved aside to allow the little terrorists to flow through the door, I spotted the drape of a long, red cape against her well-rounded hip and grinned.

As the kids filed out of the room, Lori went to put the infant into a crib across the room and Hal and I made a quick exit, plunging through the exterior door like we were being chased by slime-coated aliens.

~

*A*fter the stress of being assailed by rug-rats, Hal and I decided to walk the four blocks to *Sonny's Diner* to clear our heads. Hal was limping slightly and I had a feeling he was trying to shake off something more than residual trauma from being exposed to snotty noses and judgmental toddler gazes. But that was pure speculation on my part. Backed up by a slightly scientific knowledge of the outcome when a plastic laser gun is applied with toddler-like force to the male genitalia.

I gave him a sideways glance. "Are you okay?"

"I'm perfectly fine. Why?"

My lips twitched. "No reason. I just noticed you were limping."

He frowned but didn't respond. In fact, we walked in silence until we reached the diner and he opened the door for me. I ducked under his arm, doing a quick scan of the restaurant to see who was there.

I'd been hoping Lis would be there, schmoozing and catching up, but if I'd thought about it I would have known better.

Lis didn't eat. She subsisted mostly on air and water. I supposed there was probably some nutrition value to pollen. After all, it did come from plants.

Max hurried past, carrying two glasses of water and a pair of laminated menus pinched between her elbow and her side. "Sit wherever you want, Joey."

Hal took my arm and led me to the back wall, where a skinny guy with pimples was just finishing up wiping the tabletop. "Hey Jimmy," I said cheerfully. Jimmy Boston had been two years ahead of me in school, which made him twenty-six. I couldn't believe he still had a face full of zits at his advanced age.

"Hey, Joey." Jimmy skimmed Hal a look and turned away without another word. He'd always been socially awkward like that. I didn't know if it was the zits and greasy, too-long hair, or the fact that his mama had a long history of dabbling in Meth.

Between a horrible home life and a high bullying quotient at school, I'd always felt sorry for him. His life hadn't been an easy one. And I'd always tried to be nice in an attempt to make up for those who weren't.

I slid into the booth and Hal took the opposite bench. His sexy green gaze scoured the place, looking for heaven knew what, and then focused on the door.

I tapped his menu to try to draw his attention back to the most important thing. Lunch. "The chicken and noodles are really good here. Or the breaded pork tenderloin sandwich."

He nodded but didn't look away from the door. I wondered what he was so interested in, so I looked. There was a big, black SUV parked across the street in front of *Lester's Hardware*. "Is that...?"

Hal nodded. "Maybe we should go..."

Max suddenly appeared at the table, giving us a weary smile. "What can I get you two?"

"I'll just have the soup," Hal told her, barely looking away from the window as he spoke to Max.

"I'll have the chicken and noodles, please. Just water to drink."

Max looked at Hal. "Something to drink?"

He shook his head and then blinked, looking up at Max. "Do you have any more of that banana cream pie?"

"One slice," Max said, grinning.

I'd gotten excited when he asked the question but I deflated at her response, sighing dramatically.

"I'll take the pie too," Hal told her.

I pulled my phone out and checked emails for a few minutes, irrationally irritated at my PI. I was glad he was with me, but I was starting to worry that I wasn't going to get another slice of Max's pie until he went back to Indianapolis.

Oh well, I thought. I could always order a pie all for myself if I needed to. I couldn't replace the feelings I had, having Hal's protection and...other things...around.

The bell over the front door jangled and I looked up from my phone. My pulse spiked. "Dangit."

Hal reached across the table and patted my arm. "Don't say anything. He's just trying to harass you. Don't let him know he's having an effect."

Easier said than done, I thought. But I hated Cox enough to make the effort. If only to cause him frustration. I looked up and forced a smile as he approached the table.

"Ms. Fulle. Mr. Amity."

Hal and I nodded, remaining mute.

Cox stood awkwardly at our table, his gaze hostile. "You've been very busy."

I flinched. It hadn't occurred to me the man would have us followed. I'd been naïve. Of course he would follow us. He believed I knew where the magical "something" was he thought my parents had hidden.

I opened my mouth to say something biting but Hal clasped my hand in his, giving it a warning squeeze. I was momentarily distracted by the warm strength in that hand and Hal spoke before I could.

"Miss Fulle has told you she doesn't know

anything. If you've been tailing her you're interfering with her Constitutional rights."

Cox snorted as if the very idea of a Constitution was ridiculous. "Ms. Fulle is a person of interest in my investigation whether she likes it or not."

Heads turned in our direction from the tables and booths around us. I'd hoped the general hum of conversation would protect us from nosy diners, but I should have known better. The people in that diner knew the moment somebody new came inside. They'd taken Hal's measure immediately, their speculative gazes reflecting a keen interest in his presence there.

I figured the rumor mill had been torn between assumptions that he was my new boyfriend and conspiracy theories that he had something to do with the government and my parents' death.

Option number two was about to take precedence. News of Cox's statement would spread through the town like wildfire in a drought.

I silently cursed Cox's very public harassment.

"I told you I don't know anything and I don't," I informed him angrily, despite Hal's grip on my hand. "If you don't leave me alone I'm going to get a lawyer."

"And what?" Cox asked, laughing meanly. "Sue the U.S. government?"

A soft gasp sounded behind me and I could feel additional gazes sliding our way.

Hal squeezed my hand so hard it hurt and then

released it. "Mr. Cox, can I speak with you outside please?"

Cox narrowed his gaze on my PI and then shook his head. "I don't think so, Mr. Amity." He looked at me again, poking his finger against the table. "I'm not letting up until you help me find what your parents stole, Ms. Fulle." He lifted his hands. "All you need to do is cooperate. If you truly don't know where it is then you have nothing to lose."

"I don't even know *what* it is, Mr. Cox."

His jaw tightened as he looked down at me. "Then you shouldn't mind if we..."

"Excuse me." Max stuck a bony elbow into Cox's gut and he jumped back as if he'd been touched by a live wire. She settled our lunches onto the table and turned to him. "If you're here to eat you need to take a seat. My customers don't come in here to be harassed."

Cox seemed to be considering sliding into the booth next to me but Max crossed her arms over her chest and gave him the evil eye.

He finally laughed as if he didn't care and jabbed a finger in my direction. "I'll be in touch, Ms. Fulle."

The entire diner watched him walk away and, as he pushed the door open they cheered. Cox stiffened with anger at the obvious snub. I would have smiled if tears weren't sliding down my cheeks.

"Can I get you anything else, honey?" Max's voice was gentle. She put a hand on my shoulder as I shook my head, sniffling.

"Okay. Just let me know."

She left and a beat later conversation started back up around us. I put my head in my hands and tried to regain my equilibrium. The chicken and noodles I'd been looking forward to eating no longer held any appeal. I pushed the plate away.

Hal didn't say anything. He simply pushed the plate with his banana cream pie over in front of me. I looked up, surprised and pleased. "I can't eat your pie," I told him in a water-logged voice. Though I absolutely could, given even the slightest encouragement.

"I got it for you. I noticed how disappointed you were when I got the last piece before."

Fresh tears filled my eyes and I swiped at them, embarrassed. "That's really nice..."

"No. I owe you that pie. Just eat it. Maybe it will take the Cox stink out of your day."

Despite myself, I barked out a laugh.

The man was almost too good to be true. I wondered if he was genuine. Then a beat later I realized I didn't care.

I had pie.

So, I put my head down and started shoveling it into my mouth.

CHAPTER FOURTEEN

*D*espite Hal's earlier statement that I could pay for his meals, he insisted on paying for lunch. I was picking at my chicken and noodles, which, despite the pie and Cox's intrusion into my life, I'd managed to mostly eat, when Reverend Smythe from the Lutheran Church stopped by my table.

He gave me a serene smile. "Hello, Joey."

I quickly wiped broth off my lips. "Reverend Smythe. How are you?"

He indicated the opposite bench. "May I?"

"Of course, sit."

Hal caught my eye and pointed toward the door, indicating that he'd wait for me outside.

I pushed my plate to the side and leaned my elbows on the table, giving the Reverend my full attention. "I hope you're not here to yell at me for not coming to church."

He laughed and I grinned to show him I was kidding.

"No. I understand your world was shaken when you lost your parents. Sometimes that leads to questioning."

With Cox's recent attack still foremost on my mind, his statement alarmed me slightly. "Questioning what?"

"Why did God let this happen?" He shrugged. "That sort of thing. Perfectly understandable."

I didn't respond. In the days after their deaths I *had* wondered just exactly that. But I hated to admit it to the Reverend. And, if I was being totally honest with myself, it wasn't a new suspicion of God's motives that was keeping me from attending Sunday services. It was more a fear of how people would look at me. If my parents had been guilty of the things Cox and crew had accused them of, did I deserve the peace and comfort provided within the church's walls?

Reverend Smythe watched me carefully, his kind brown gaze seeming to pierce my skin and drive right into my heart, assessing my inclinations.

I finally shook my head. "I'm okay."

"I knew your parents for five years, Joey. They were good people. Don't let that terrible man convince you otherwise."

To my horror, hot tears filled my eyes again. I sniffled, nodding. "I'm trying. It's not easy."

"I know it isn't."

I glanced toward the window, seeing Hal leaning against a street light, talking on his cell phone. I wondered who he was talking to.

"Well...I know you're busy so I won't keep you."

I turned back to the man across from me. "No, I'm glad you stopped to say hi."

"I did. But that's not the only reason I came over." He leaned closer and lowered his voice. "I understand you've been asking Buck Mitzner a bunch of questions about what happened on your property."

"I...I know he's been helping you out at the church." And that would naturally predispose the kindly Reverend to take Buck's side.

The Reverend seemed to dismiss my excuse with a wave of his hand. "That's not why I'm here. I get why you and Arno might suspect him..."

"Arno spoke to you about Buck?"

"He did. I told him what I'm going to tell you. I shouldn't tell you, of course, but I feel as if I have to. Buck doesn't need any more stress. He's..." The Reverend frowned. "Well, let's just say he's fighting something right now."

I felt my eyes go wide. *Fighting something*? Of course my first thought was a disease of some kind. "Cancer?"

"No, my dear." He sighed. "But ultimately it might be worse."

I was intrigued. My mind spun over the possibilities. "What are you trying to tell me?"

"Buck was with me until very late the night of the...erm...event in your woods."

"Oh. How late?"

"Until well after Midnight. He'd come to a...meeting...at eight o'clock. The meeting shut down around ten, it ran very late, and then he came to my office and prayed with me for a while. After that we chatted."

"Okay. That's good to know. Unfortunately, Arno hasn't given me a time of death so I don't know if Buck was..."

"He wasn't. Arno believes the poor creature in that chipper died around eleven pm. It couldn't have been Buck."

I had to admit I was a little disappointed. Buck fit the bill perfectly for a murderer. Despite the nagging thought that he'd have to be exceptionally stupid to use one of his own chippers for the job. "Thanks for letting me know," I told him.

As Reverend Smythe stood up, I reached out and touched his hand. "What kind of meeting was it?"

"I'm afraid I can't tell you that, child."

Putting it together with the other information he'd offered me, his non-answer was all the answer I needed. Buck had to be going to the *Alcoholics Anonymous* meetings at the church. Given my past experiences with the man, that made total sense.

But as I watched Reverend Smythe move carefully toward the door, stopping to clasp hands and speak briefly to several people along the way, I recognized that Hal and I would have to scratch a key suspect from our list.

And that didn't take me to my happy place.

When I got outside, Hal was speaking to Arno. He disconnected and straightened away from the light pole. "All set?"

I nodded. "Did Arno have any new information for us?" I fell into step beside him and we walked the four blocks back to where we'd left his car.

"He did. He said Devon Little wasn't the body in that chipper. The DNA isn't a match."

I considered the information, relieved as well as disappointed. I was glad the body wasn't someone I knew, but that meant we still didn't know who it was. "I guess that's good news," I murmured half to myself.

"It certainly is for Mr. Little," Hal told me with a grin.

"Yeah. But if it wasn't him, then where is he? And why would he disappear?"

"I've been thinking about that," Hal told me. "Was he a person of interest with the FBI too?"

I shook my head. "Not that I know of. But to tell you the truth I don't know why he wasn't. He was my dad's right-hand man. He knew everything about the business and he had a hand in all of it. In fact, given his personality and malleable moral fiber, I'd be more inclined to think he'd be the one to do something squiggy if something squiggy was done."

"His disappearance seems to suggest you might be right."

"Unless something's happened to him." I frowned. "Just because he wasn't in that chipper doesn't mean he wasn't a target too."

"Agreed." Hal clicked to unlock his car.

I waited while he opened the door for me and then slipped inside. As Hal pulled the SUV away from the curb I asked. "Where to next?"

He glanced at me. "Do you know where Buck Mitzner lives?"

"I do." Frowning, I considered what Reverend Smythe had told me. "But I don't think he's involved in this."

"Why not?"

I told Hal about my conversation with the Reverend.

He listened carefully, taking the shaded twists and turns of *Country Road 57* at a sedate speed. But when I'd finished he didn't look convinced.

"You still think Buck's involved?"

"I don't *not* think that."

I stared at him, my brain screaming in pain as I tried to untwist his statement for its actual meaning. "Okay, how about we try that again. Do you think Buck is involved in the chipper murder?"

"I think the Reverend is probably a very good man who's predisposed to think the best of his flock. And, having met the man, I think the idea of Buck praying for two hours is a stretch."

I felt my eyes go round. "I can't believe you think Reverend Smythe is lying."

"I didn't say that. But my experience is that sometimes even the most honest people will obfuscate if they believe it's helping someone who they perceive doesn't deserve what they're facing. There's at least a small possibility that's the case here. Enough of a chance that it's worth looking into Buck."

I sighed. "Okay. But I want to go on record as thinking it's a waste of time."

"Duly noted."

We came to a sharp turn in the road and Hal eased the speed down a few notches as we approached. To our right, the woods pressed against the edge of the road and to our left, the landscape fell away to a stunning and intimidating vista of rocks, trees and a plunging decline. *CR57* had many such spectacular views. As a result, three-foot-wide gravel shoulders graced its entire curvy length to accommodate looky-loos.

I let my gaze slide over the breathtaking vista, barely noting the low-slung muscle car parked on the opposite shoulder, its driver no doubt enjoying the beautiful panorama. I didn't even have time to notice the car was facing the wrong direction before its brake lights went dark and it surged across the other lane and into ours.

I screamed. We were going to collide.

Hal's foot slammed down on the brake and he jerked the wheel toward the far side of the road, no doubt hoping to pull around the other car. I hit the shoulder strap of my seatbelt and pain stabbed through me as it locked into place.

In the blink of an eye I had a new terror, as Hal's SUV headed straight for the guardrail, and the steep and deadly drop beyond.

He fought the wheel as the big car, unsteady because of its height to width ratio and the curve in the road, started to wobble and fishtail.

Somehow, he managed to slow and ease to a stop. Turning to me, he must have been alarmed by my white face. "You okay?"

I slid a finger under the shoulder strap, wincing. "I think so. But I'm definitely going to have a bruise."

He opened his mouth to respond but never got the chance. A horrendous crunching noise preceded a violent wrenching of the car sideways, toward the looming precipice.

Hal swore, turning in his seat to find the same muscle car, windows too dark to see inside, backing up to hit us again.

"Hold on!" Hal yelled and he wrenched the wheel toward the road, hitting the gas as our attacker lunged forward again and caught the outside corner of the bumper.

The SUV skidded sideways on the gravel and the left, rear bumper crashed into the metal guardrail to the sound of crunching and groaning.

The tires spun wildly on the loose rock and the car skipped sideways, finally catching on the asphalt and surging forward as the muscle car shot off the mark after us.

Hal's big hands on the steering wheel were white around the knuckles, his gaze alternating between watching the curving road ahead and the muscle car surging forward in our wake.

He came up on another sharp turn and I sucked air, bracing myself on the dashboard as he swerved out into the other lane so he could take the turn without braking. I prayed no cars were coming from the opposite direction because we were blinded by the curve and definitely in position for a head-on collision.

The SUV's oversized tires screamed beneath us and we started to skid. Hal was forced to slow to keep from losing control.

The muscle car took the opportunity to roar forward and hurtle into the back bumper again.

For a horrible moment there was a dragging motion and the SUV slowed.

Hal's face lost color and the engine of the car behind us roared, the wide, flat nose weaving back and forth and dragging us with it. Like a shark trying to rip its prey from a hook.

"He's caught on our bumper!" Hal said in a voice that made my stomach twist with fear.

We were all probably going to die. And if Hal and I managed to survive the deadly fall to the rocky floor far below, we'd surely be crushed by the weight of the muscle car smashing down on top of us.

"Do something!" I screamed in a total panic. As soon as I yelled at him I regretted it. I was being unreasonable. Why should I expect him to fix a problem I couldn't begin to find a solution to?

But Hal wasn't paying attention to me anyway. His quick brain had apparently already formed a plan. As we headed straight for a massive tree growing just beyond the guard rail, he threw one last look at the car jerking along behind us and grasped the emergency brake. He yelled, "crash position!" and slammed his foot down on the brake pedal as he wrenched the emergency brake up. The SUV squealed, its back-end swerving and its tires sending smoke up to obscure the car behind us.

For a long moment I didn't think his maneuver had accomplished anything. We were still heading toward the massive tree, almost certainly to our deaths if we hit the tree head-on, or to a fiery end at the bottom of the ravine if we glanced off and sailed through the guard rail into the abyss. But then there was a wrenching sound and the muscle car jerked free, barreling even more quickly toward the tree as the driver clearly fought for control.

I screamed and tucked my head between my knees, saying a prayer that my death would be quick and painless.

The tires squealed beneath us again and the engine roared, a loud clanking sound settling in to follow us down the road. After ten seconds and no crash, I slowly lifted my head. We were back in our lane and barreling down *Country Road 57*.

I dared a quick glance behind us and saw only empty road. "He's gone?"

Hal nodded, his jaw tight and his hands squeezing the steering wheel so tightly it creaked.

"Oh my god," I moaned, wrapping my arms around my stomach. "I think I'm going to be sick."

Hal skimmed me a quick glance then, some of the intensity leeching from his green eyes. "You might want to wait on that until we get to your house," he told me.

I looked through the windshield, finally seeing where we were. It was less than a mile until the turn onto my road.

We'd made it.

Some of the terror clawing at my stomach eased and I found it easier to breathe.

Until the adrenaline started to drain away. Then I started to shake so hard I almost vibrated off the seat.

CHAPTER FIFTEEN

*M*y dog was an immobile, furry weight across my lap. Where usually she'd lay her big head on my thigh when I sat on the couch, Caphy had apparently decided I needed even more support and had draped her big body entirely over me.

She wasn't wrong.

I dug my shaky hands deep into her soft fur and massaged, enjoying the soft groans of pleasure and the way her pretty green eyes narrowed as I worked my way down her body. Slowly but surely my ministrations were calming me down.

I'd been a wild-eyed, vibrating mess when Hal had pulled up in front of my house. He'd had to take the keys from me because I couldn't hold my hands still long enough to insert one into the lock and open the front door.

When I got inside Caphy leaped at me, tongue

lolling and tail whipping the air with manic pleasure. I dropped my purse and fell to my knees, burying my face in her fur and giving into tears as she scraped her wide, pink tongue over my arm.

Caphy calmed immediately, falling back on years of experience soothing me when I hit the edge of my emotional reserves.

I felt Hal's hand on my arm. "Come on, Joey. Let's get you inside and onto the couch. You can rest while I make you some tea."

I let myself be drawn to my feet and moved like a zombie toward the living room. After the terror in the car and the subsequent emotional response, I was starting to feel drained and numb.

"She's all yours, girl," Hal told my dog, scratching her head before leaving us for the kitchen. Even through my emotional fog, I followed his movements in the kitchen, hearing the clank of the teapot, the rush of water and the thrum of it hitting the bottom of the pot, and then the clinking of spoon and mug as he prepped my tea.

Then silence.

I closed my eyes, focusing on the feeling of soft fur in my fingers and the reassuring weight of my devoted pibl.

Hal's voice broke my reverie and, for a brief moment I thought he was talking to me. But he was far away and his voice sounded strangely hushed.

He was telling someone about the ambush on the road.

I tried not to listen because just hearing him describe it again brought panic oozing back up.

Caphy whined, frantically licking my fingers in an effort to calm me.

"Shhh," I hushed her softly. I took a deep breath and tried to calm back down again.

"I think you need to come over," Hal said, his voice firm.

My eyes shot open.

"Okay," he said in a half-angry tone. Then silence.

The teapot whistled sharply and cut off with a dying whine as Hal apparently grabbed it off the stove.

A moment later his footsteps sounded on the hallway floor and I closed my eyes again, pretending I was unaware.

I wasn't sure why I was pretending, but I was going on pure instinct at that point.

Caphy's tail slapped against the couch cushions and I felt Hal's presence in the room. I opened my eyes.

He handed me my favorite mug, which said "The most dangerous part of a pit bull" and showed a picture of a wagging tail.

"Thanks," I said, taking the mug. It was steaming hot and the aroma rising from the liquid was soothing and sweet.

"I added honey to ward off shock. Just in case."

I didn't sip from it, preferring to hold it a moment, warming my hands.

Hal sat down across from me and gave me an encouraging smile. "Drink your tea, Joey."

A surge of resistance rose up inside me. I suddenly didn't want to drink the tea. I was mad at him for sneaking that phone call in the kitchen and I couldn't help wondering who he'd been talking to. "I don't think I want it. But thanks."

"It will help relax you," he said, eyeing me carefully.

I gave a quick jerk of my head. Caphy scraped her big tongue over my leg, leaving a giant wet spot on my shorts.

"Who were you talking to?" I asked him, trying to keep my voice neutral.

He hesitated just long enough to make me believe he was going to lie. "Arno. I told him about the...incident...on the road."

I held the tea and stared at him. He stared back. "Is he coming over?"

"He can't. He says he's too busy. He wants us to come into the station later today or in the morning to give him all the details."

I wasn't sure if Hal was telling me the truth or not. What he said sounded like Arno. He'd be feeling all threatened and manly about Hal's intrusion in his case. But at the same time he'd feel grateful Hal had managed to keep us alive. He was most likely in a quandary.

Like I was.

I'd had trouble trusting people all my life. It probably had something to do with the way my parents ran their business, like a giant, special secret that they kept just between the two of them. I'd always envied them their secret. It seemed to bring them closer together. They were like an island in the world. Alone and happy.

But an island for two had left me out in the cold.

So, I'd also hated them for their secret. I blinked, realizing it was the first time I'd ever admitted that to myself. I'd always been a little jealous of my parents' relationship because it sometimes felt as if it excluded me.

And even now, after they'd been gone almost two years, I was still clinging to that resentment.

I frowned, saddened by my own feelings.

"Are you okay? Is there anything I can do for you?"

I skimmed Hal a look, the scales of suspicion falling away. I saw again the handsome and serious man who'd come to my rescue when I'd asked and had done everything he could to help me, and keep my dog and me safe while he was there.

And I was repaying him with suspicion.

I was suddenly ashamed.

I gave him a smile that I hoped was sincere. "I'm good. Just feeling a little drained and freaked out."

He inclined his dark head. "Totally understandable. Why don't you try to rest? I'll keep watch."

I lifted the mug. "Thank you for this. You're right.

It might help me rest." To show him I meant it, I lifted the mug and took a sip.

"Good. I'm just going out to look at the car. See if I can strap that bumper on until I have a chance to get it into the shop. Will you be okay in here with Caphy?"

I swallowed another sip, amazed at how good it tasted. "We're perfect. Go ahead and do what you need to do."

"Okay." He stared down at me for another moment, some undefined emotion flaring in his sexy gaze, and then nodded. "I'll just be outside. And I'll leave the door open. If you need me..."

"I'll call," I assured him.

I took a couple more sips of tea and then, as I felt my muscles begin to relax, I set it on the table and lay down, pulling my dog close so she was draped along my front. I wrapped my arms around her and, with a shaky sigh, drifted off to sleep.

~

The sun was beaming in the window when I came awake. I was drowsy and felt like I'd been hit by a truck.

That thought brought my eyes fully open as I remembered I *had* been hit. Several times.

By a shark-nosed car.

Caphy was no longer on the couch with me so I

sat up, yawning widely, and stretched, looking around for her.

She barked happily, the sound coming from outside. It was probably her barking that had brought me awake.

I shoved at the throw I didn't remember pulling over myself and pushed to my feet. The front door was closed but Hal had opened the window with Caphy smears all over it, allowing a warm, sweetly scented breeze to dance over me as I looked outside.

The pibl ran in enthusiastic circles, barking up at the sky, as a couple of massive turkey vultures orbited the pond. I smiled. She'd never understood the concepts of air and ground...and the reality that she couldn't catch a bird that flew by high over her head.

A voice pulled my attention away from Caphy and I frowned when I found Hal, leaning against his battered SUV, arms crossed over his chest and a scowl on his face.

A woman in a form-fitting light gray suit stood a couple of feet away from him, her back to me. I couldn't see her face or hear what they were saying, but I could see that she was lean and attractive in a very athletic way that I would never be able to master.

She stood with her hands on her narrow hips, her shapely legs splayed in battle stance, and one dainty foot in a two-inch high heel that matched her suit tapping against the drive as if she were irritated.

Before I gave my actions any thought, I was storming to the door and yanking it open.

Both of them turned when I came outside. Both of them frowned as if I were an unwelcome addition to their little twosome. And both of them made a little sound of alarm when I took the top step without looking down and caught the toe of my flip flop on the concrete. Arms flailing wildly, I stumbled down three very hard steps and crumpled into an achy heap at the bottom.

Well, I thought as they hurried over to help and I tried to fold myself into the fetal position and hide. *I always have known how to make an entrance.*

"Are you all right, Joey?"

My PI always seemed to be asking me that. I suddenly found it irritating.

"I'm fine," I snapped at him, jerking my arm away. "I just want to sit here a while."

Hal tried to clasp my arm and help me off the ground. I jerked my arm away. "Just give me a minute, please!"

The woman stared down at me with bright blue eyes that were filled with amusement. A dense fan of dark gold lashes framed her pretty gaze. She pursed perfectly shaped pink lips and reached up to tuck a strand of dark gold hair behind one ear, her cute, pixy hairstyle flaring out in perfect flips around her perfect head.

Her lips twitched when I yelled at Hal and that made me dislike her immensely.

I looked up at him. "I'm sorry. I slept really deeply. I must still be a little drowsy."

He nodded. "You need to clean that up."

For the first time I looked down and saw that I'd badly skinned one knee, the blood running down my shin.

"Ugh." I stood up, ignoring the woman's offered hand of support. Then I fixed her with a look that I hoped regained at least a sliver of the dignity I'd thrown out the window when I'd toppled down the stairs and offered her my hand. "I'm Joey Fulle."

"Prudence Frect. My friends call me Pru."

Of course they do, I couldn't help thinking.

She shook my hand and gave me a tight smile. "I understand you've been on a bit of a wild ride lately."

I looked at Hal, lifting a questioning brow.

He flushed slightly. "I'm sorry, Joey. I would have run it by you but you were sleeping and I didn't want to wake you up. I invited Pru...erm...Prudence here to help us figure out what's going on."

A scowl crawled across my face and I did nothing to stop it. "You hired another investigator without asking me first?"

Hal didn't get a chance to respond. She cut him off. "I'm not a PI. I'm FBI."

Both eyebrows jerked upward. "You hired one of Cox's cronies?"

"Nobody hired me," Prudence said in a voice tinged with impatience. "I'm here as Hal's friend."

I wasn't sure I liked that any better.

"Pru isn't a fan of Cox," Hal told me, his manner unapologetic. "And to tell you the truth, with two attempts on your life already and an unsolved murder, I thought the best way I could keep you safe was to consult with Pru."

I carefully modulated my voice, trying to mask some of the irritability in it. "What have the two of you figured out?"

"Pru knows a bit about Cox's investigation into your parents," he told me.

I let that sink in for a moment and then nodded. I looked at Miss Pru Frect. *God help me.* "We might as well go inside. I need to feed my dog and then myself." My stomach growled and I flushed with embarrassment. Shoving it away, I whistled for Caphy and started up the steps.

After all, once you've proven to your natural enemies that you're about as graceful as a hippopotamus in ballet class, there was nowhere to go but up.

CHAPTER SIXTEEN

"Talk to me," I told Pru as I settled into a chair across from her.

Hal placed a plate with a delicious looking burger in front of me and put catsup and mustard in the center of the table. "Eat up before it gets cold."

I plucked a crispy sweet potato fry off the plate and nibbled it, nearly moaning with delight as the sweet and salty flavor burst over my tongue.

I was starting to think Hal had a magic bag with an endless supply of groceries in it, ala Mary Poppins. "Where do you keep pulling this food from?"

He arched a dark brow at me. "When was the last time you looked in your freezer?"

My lips twitched. "Did you just answer a question with a question?"

"Do you really want me to answer that?"

We shared a grin and I felt my equilibrium returning.

Pru looked at her plate and I pictured her rejecting the food. I spent a gleeful moment wondering how Hal would take her rejection of his cooking. She was probably one of those annoying rabbit food females. You know the type. The ones who subsist on grass and dandelions with vinegar for dressing and think eating dessert is akin to chomping rat poison.

But she surprised me by putting a healthy dose of both catsup and mustard onto her burger and then arranging pickles in vast amounts over the condiments. Pressing the bun down on top and cutting the burger in half, Pru frowned. "Where do I start?"

I swallowed my bite of burger, which was every bit as delicious as the fry had been. "How about two years before they died. Because that's when I remember seeing Cox for the first time."

Pru nodded. "You're close. Actually, it was about eighteen months. I remember because that was when the Monet disappeared."

Hal sat down with his own plate, which overflowed with two burgers and a mountain of fries.

"Monet?" I asked her.

"Yes. That was what brought Cox to your doorstep. The theft was tracked to *Deer Hollow* and, since your parents had a shadow business selling expensive items to wealthy buyers around the world, they were the obvious target for the investigation."

I held up my hands, licking one of them when I noticed the smear of mustard painting the tip. "Hold on. Shadow business?" I shook my head. "Never mind that for the moment. Let's go back to the Monet. Tell me about it."

She stopped with her burger halfway to her mouth and stared at me, clearly not used to being interrupted.

Funny how I didn't give a dang. "I have a reason for asking."

Pru took her bite, chewing slowly, and sipped her water before responding. "It was a little-known painting by Monet entitled, *Blue Boats*. The painting was an earlier one and it inspired the painting he eventually called, *Red Boats*. Part of his *Argenteuil* collection. But Monet didn't like the way the painting turned out so he disposed of it in a fit of temper. A friend begged to be allowed to save it from the trash, promising never to reveal its existence to anyone. Apparently, Monet reluctantly allowed it to be retrieved. Nobody knew anything about the painting until decades later, when Monet's friend, a guy named Alexandre Dubois, who at the time was desperate for money and very ill, tried to sell it on the street. Fortunately for the art world, the man who bought it recognized its value and placed it in his own, private collection, which was passed down within his family for several generations before it was stolen."

"How was it stolen," Hal asked.

"I don't know all the details, but apparently it happened in transit to the *Art Institute of Chicago*." She made a face. "Ironic since the family had refused to allow it into a museum until that point. And a little sad."

"How was it traced here?" I asked.

"That's a little trickier. Cox had a source who he refused to name. That source apparently saw the painting mixed in with several other items that were going to be delivered to your parents' auction. It was wrapped but the source was curious because he'd heard about the theft and he opened the wrapping to look."

"Why didn't he just take the painting to the police?" Hal asked.

"I think Cox was hoping to catch the thief and planned to follow the painting to its ultimate destination." Pru shrugged. "Like I said, the details of that part of this are murky at best. Cox keeps his information close."

I set my burger down, my appetite gone. "That doesn't make any sense. My parents only auctioned off farm equipment. They didn't have the connections to dispose of a valuable and very hot painting."

"That's where the shadow business comes in."

"My parents weren't involved in anything illegal. If Cox could have proven that he already would have." Heat infused my face and my hands shook with anger. I was sick of people disparaging the motives of my dead parents.

Pru lifted a hand. "Maybe that wasn't a good choice of words. I don't mean shadowy. I just mean it was a side business that was lightly connected to the auction. Your parents were go-betweens for the sale of precious goods between private investors."

"What does that even mean?"

She nibbled on a fry while she seemed to be considering how to respond. Finally, she picked up her napkin, wiping her fingers. "Sometimes people sold things that had been in their families for a long time. Sales they didn't want to go public for whatever reason." She must have seen me bristle because she quickly clarified. "Not necessarily illegal reasons. Many times, there are family concerns. Sometimes it's purely a personal need for privacy." She shrugged.

"And my parents were selected for this why?"

"Despite what you believe, they did have connections, Joey. Lots of them. With people in the right economic spheres. And they had the ability to perform the private exchange of funds or goods."

"They had their own plane for private deliveries," Hal added, nodding.

Despite my resistance, Pru's story was starting to make sense. Especially when I looked back at my parents' practices.

But it all fell apart with the stolen painting. "My parents would have known the painting was stolen," I told her. "They wouldn't have taken it on."

"Actually, I don't think they did take it on. We have no record that they either requested or accepted the item. In fact, though I can't get Cox to consider the possibility, I believe it's entirely possible that the thief planted the painting in their warehouse to point the finger at them for the theft."

"And then took the painting out after it was spotted," Hal said. "That makes a lot of sense. What better way to take the heat off than to give the world a plausible thief whose practices would make disposal of the painting much easier."

I still didn't like it. "That would all depend on someone seeing the painting in the warehouse," I argued. "And even Cox's informer said it was wrapped. That seems like a real risk to me."

"I agree," Pru told me. "Which is why I think the informant might be the thief."

Hal and I stared at her for a long moment. Then I leaned forward, excited. "If that's true the problem's solved. You just need to make Cox give up his informant."

Pru laughed. "You *have* met him, right?"

"This is important enough you could go over his head," Hal said.

"You don't think I've tried that? Cox is bulletproof. He's got wings in the organization. Aspirations and sponsors. They'd never believe me over him. Besides..." She threw me an apologetic smile. "They have a perfect scapegoat in your parents. They have no incentive at all to rock that boat."

"That blue boat," I murmured, miserable.

"What happened to the painting? Has it been recovered?" Hal asked.

"No. And that brings us to the present problem."

She swung her gaze back to me. "We think your parents tried to find the real thief, Joey. And maybe they did. Maybe they threatened to expose the person if he didn't cough up the painting. And maybe that got them killed."

I swallowed hard, my mind spinning. I'd often thought about whether my parents' death was really an accident. There had been speculation at the time. Even through my grief I'd noticed the whispered conversations that died quickly away when I walked into a room. And the way people looked at me, as if I might be holding a dangerous secret close and they wanted to warn me not to tell anyone.

I'd thought at the time I was just being paranoid. But suddenly I wondered if I was. "You're saying my parents' crash wasn't an accident?"

"It's possible."

"Did the FBI find any proof of that?" Hal asked.

"Nothing definitive. But nobody's come up yet with a plausible explanation for how that rock got on the runway."

And just in time to take advantage of a storm that had rolled in as my parents landed, utilizing a driving rain and the subsequent lack of visibility. It wasn't very sophisticated sabotage, if that's what it was, but it had been effective. "It wouldn't take any special knowledge to crash a plane with a rock on the runway," I told Pru.

"Exactly. Which means our pool of suspects widens considerably."

"So, other than Joey, who is Cox looking at?"

Pru shook her head. "He's not. That's the problem. He's convinced Joey knows where that painting is."

"And he thinks I killed my own parents?" I shrieked unbecomingly.

"Not necessarily. He's working off the simplest scenario. That your parents died in a freak accident and that you're protecting their memory by not admitting they stole the painting."

Hal sighed. "It's plausible enough. The rock could have been carried there by kids. And clearly Joey is protective of her parents."

I glared at him, my pulse spiking with anger. "You're buying Cox's theory then?"

"I'm not buying anything, Joey. I'm investigating this along with you."

His answer didn't make me feel any better. "I can't believe it."

"Look," he said, lifting his hands off the table. "I'm not going to do you any good at all if I let myself buy into your concept of your parents without any evidence to back it up. Of course, you believe they're innocent. They were your parents and you loved them. But you said yourself they didn't always include you in things. It's possible they did some things that were slightly above the law. Maybe even for the right reasons. The only way to clear their names is to shine a light on all the evidence and discover some that proves their innocence."

What he was saying made sense. But I wasn't feeling reasonable. I'd thought Hal was firmly on my side. And then Prudence Frect showed up and he was suddenly doubting whether I really knew my parents or not. Or worse, whether I'd stolen an...erm...stolen painting.

I stood up so quickly my chair tipped backward, slamming against the floor. Caphy jumped up with a yelp, scurrying away with her tail tucked. I glared at him, ignoring the miserable expression on his handsome face. "I guess I'm on my own in this then. Like I always am. You might as well leave with Prudence. You're fired."

"Joey..."

I spun on my heel and stalked out of the kitchen, heading out into the still warm evening. Caphy was right on my heels. I took off running around the house, not even knowing where I was headed.

It didn't matter anyway. I just needed to be alone. I told myself the spike of pain in the vicinity of my heart was because I was mad at Hal. Not because I'd thought I finally had someone I could count on and he'd let me down.

They always let me down.

And they always believed my parents were criminals.

I ran until the stitch in my side made me stop. Then I stumbled forward, panting and sore, toward the only place I could still feel my parents as they'd always been.

To the spot where my parents had breathed their last breaths.

And plunged me into the dual nightmare of doubt and loneliness.

~

A light rain misted my face and weighted down my hair. I tugged it off my face and twisted it at the back of my neck, then rubbed the moisture off my face with the hem of my shirt.

Thunder rumbled softly in the distance and I watched the jagged play of lightning cut the quickly approaching clouds. The thick, iron-gray cloud cover was pulling the light from the day, dragging an early nighttime into place. I stared at the long, unbroken runway, trying to picture it as it had been before they'd died.

The grass was up to my thighs, dotted with thistle and milkweed and untamed where it had once been carefully manicured.

Somewhere in that tangle of vegetation were large chunks of refuse from the crash. Remnants of the worst night of my life, which I couldn't bear to remove.

Behind me was the big, metal outbuilding where the two-person Cessna had been housed. And the office where my father took care of all the details involved in having a plane. A large metal tank sat rusting beside the building, still full of aviation fuel.

I had memories from when I was a kid, probably around nine or ten, of sitting in the shade of the hangar building watching my dad fuel his fast little plane for a trip. When I'd been a kid they'd taken me with them on their frequent trips.

As I got older they'd chosen to leave me behind.

A rebel thought intruded on the memory. *Why had they stopped bringing me along? Was it because I was old enough to ask uncomfortable questions?*

I shoved doubt away. If I gave into it at all, I'd surely join the rest of the world in doubting them.

And I was all they had left.

Caphy lifted her head and gave a worried look at the distant sky, shivering against my hip as another low groan of thunder rolled through the clouds.

"We'll go back soon, girl. I promise."

The truth was I was afraid to go back home.

Afraid Hal would be there and almost more afraid he wouldn't.

A moment later I lost the choice of going back. The sky opened up, turning the mist into a thunderous downpour that pelted painfully against my skin.

I jumped up and ran toward the hangar, praying the door wasn't still dead-bolted. I couldn't remember if I'd locked the place back up after my parents' death.

That time was all a blur.

Fortunately, it wasn't locked. I shoved one side of the big, sliding doors open just enough for Caphy and me to squeeze through and pushed it closed again as the rain forced its way inside, like a heat-seeking missile.

The torrent banged against the door and the ceiling, creating a jarring sound that made me want to cover my ears. I shivered violently and turned to the small door on the sidewall.

My father's office.

I wasn't sure I could go in there. I hadn't been inside since his death.

Another teeth clacking shiver made up my mind for me. I would just duck inside and grab the aviator jacket he always kept in there. And then I'd get right back out.

Caphy's head lifted and her gaze shot to the office door. She gave a little bark, her tail wagging half-heartedly.

Tears burned behind my lids. She thought my father would be in that tiny office.

I hurried over and grabbed the knob, taking a deep breath to give myself strength, and then pulled it open.

Standing on the threshold, I stared at the sight in front of me. I narrowed my gaze, trying to remember if the room had been that way when I'd last seen it.

Surely not.

It looked like someone had tossed the place. Except not really. The drawers of my father's antique wooden desk were closed and the contents presumably still intact. The painting of my father's pretty little Cessna, which my mom had done for him as a wedding present, was still hanging on the wall across from his desk where he could see it. And the two remote control cars my dad and I had raced across the hangar were still there.

The framed pictures of me and my mom and of all three of us together were still in their spots on the wall. And the one, small window was intact, the dusty shade still tucked up at the top because my father had loved to watch the sun come up from his little office.

The thought made my eyes tear up. I shoved it away, tired of feeling melancholy. It was well past time I proved my parents were innocent of the things they'd been charged with.

Caphy dove happily into the mess on the floor and came up with part of a hamburger. She'd swallowed it whole before I even had time to react.

"Ew! No, girl. Heaven knows how long that's been here."

She wagged her tail and stuck her nose back in the mess. She came up with an empty French fry box. Since I'd yelled at her about the burger, she stood staring at me with the grease-saturated box in her mouth as if waiting for my permission to eat it.

"Drop it," I told her firmly.

She gave her tail a half-wag, clearly hoping I was just kidding, and then lowered her head and gacked it out on the floor.

"Good girl," I told her, scratching her between

SAM CHEEVER

the ears. "What a mess. I can't believe it's been like this for two years."

Caphy growled low and stepped forward, her body vibrating against my leg and her lips peeled back to show her teeth.

"It hasn't been," a rusty voice said from behind me.

I spun around with a yelp of surprise. "What are you doing here?"

CHAPTER SEVENTEEN

My father's old partner looked a lot the worse for wear. Devon Little was dressed in filthy clothes that hung on his once robust frame like rags on a skeleton. His graying brown hair was long and hung in greasy strings down past his chin.

A bushy mustache and a scraggly beard obscured much of his face. The round, ruddy face I remembered was transformed, his cheeks scored with deep creases and the puffiness around his eyes telling a tale of stress and weariness.

He stood straight and tall, though, and his carriage reflected a residual arrogance that had always made people trust and rely on him. As my father had.

"How are you, Joey?"

"I'm okay. What's going on, Uncle Dev? We were at your place and it was empty."

A shadow passed over his face and his bottom lip,

barely visible between the mustache and the beard, quivered slightly. It was the only sign of weakness he would show me. He clenched his hands, drawing my gaze to them. They were covered in filth and he was soaked through from the rain. "Who's the guy? He looks like a cop."

With a jolt of surprise, I saw that he was angry. "Hal? He's a private investigator from Indy. He's helping me figure out what's going on." I frowned. "What do you know about the corpse in the chipper?"

Dev's dark brown gaze hardened, but not before pain flared in the depths. "I don't know anything."

I could tell he was lying. "People are trying to kill me. If you know something about all this mess you need to tell me."

His jaw tightened and he took two, quick steps in my direction, closing the distance between us to mere inches. I winced both from surprise and from the sour stench of his body.

"You need to get out of *Deer Hollow*, Joey. I can't protect you. I'm too busy staying alive myself. But I owed it to your father to tell you to leave. It isn't safe for you here."

"I'm not going anywhere."

One of his hands snaked out and snagged my wrist, squeezing it hard. "You need to go!"

His grip was painful and I tried to pull free. "Stop it, you're hurting me!"

Caphy snarled and Dev jumped. "Down, Caphy, girl. It's all right."

My pitty growled long and low, clearly no longer trusting the man who'd brought her to me after finding her abandoned on the side of the road. The memory made my chest twist with pain. Devon Little had once been like family to us, to Caphy and me. I was no longer sure if he fit that role, but I shared my dog's distrust. "She'll stop growling if you let go of me and step back."

Dev seemed unwilling to do that. "I need you to understand."

We both went still at the unmistakable sound of a bullet being ratcheted into the chamber of a gun.

"Let her go."

I closed my eyes as a wave of relief swept me.

Uncle Dev's grip tightened for a beat and then he released me, lifting his hands over his head. "I'm no danger to her."

"Joey, come over here."

I opened my eyes, scouring my dad's former partner with a glower, and moved around the desk to Hal. Caphy trotted along with me, so close I could feel the brush of her wet fur against my leg.

Hal swept an angry glance over me as I approached. "Did he hurt you?"

I rubbed my wrist, giving my head a quick shake. I couldn't believe he was still there. I'd been so afraid I'd run him off.

He relaxed slightly. "This is Devon Little I presume?"

"Yes. He was just getting ready to tell me what's going on," I said in an uncompromising tone.

"Can I turn around? I'd like to face the man holding a gun on me."

"Turn," Hal told him, the gun pointed directly at Dev's heart. "But you can drop the victim act. You've been here all this time and you did nothing to help or protect Joey from the results of your own mess."

Uncle Dev turned slowly around, his arms still in the air. "I don't really care what you think of me, Hal the PI. But believe it or not I have been looking out for her the only way I know how."

"By hiding in the hangar?" I accused.

Devon shrugged. "I'm not proud of it but, yes. I figured getting lost was the best way to protect you. If the people looking for that painting find me they'll use whatever means they can to get me to tell them where it is, including threatening you."

"This is how you repay your old friend? By leaving his daughter on her own when your crap blows up in your face?"

Dev shook his head but didn't try to defend himself further. He probably realized there was no point. Hal was too angry to listen.

A fact that created a warm spot in my heart.

"Just tell us what you know, Dev. Who was the body in the chipper? Did you put him there?"

"I don't know who he is."

"Stop lying," Hal said in a dangerously soft voice.

"I'm not lying. I don't know his name. He's just some homeless guy. He was squatting in the woods and I think he might have moved into the cabin when I left."

"Why would the people who are after you kill a random homeless guy?" Hal asked.

"They probably thought he was me. I'm sure they tortured him to find out the location of the painting."

A deep sadness overwhelmed me, making it hard to breathe. I dragged air into my lungs and focused on Dev. "You know where the painting is?" I asked him.

Dev gave a harsh laugh. "I wish."

"If you don't know, why do they think you do?"

He gave Hal an impatient look. "How the heck do I know? Because they're crazy?"

"Okay, let's start at the beginning," Hal said, lowering the gun to his side. "Tell us how this all started."

Uncle Dev looked at the ground, his body slumping wearily. He scratched his chin through the beard and finally sighed. "I guess I might as well. Keeping quiet about it all these years hasn't helped at all." He looked up, his gaze pleading. "Do you mind if I sit down, though? I haven't had much to eat lately and I'm weak."

I thought about the partial hamburger I'd seen Caphy snarf down and frowned, feeling like my dad's old friend was still playing us for fools.

Hal inclined his head. "Keep your hands on top of the desk."

Dev dropped into my dad's worn, black leather chair. He leaned forward, putting his elbows on the desktop and sighing. If he was acting he was very good at it. "That's better. Thanks."

"Talk."

Dev shot Hal an irritated look. "Fine. Clearly you already know about the painting. About how it came into our sphere."

When Hal and I nodded, he went on.

"Your parents found out about it after it disappeared. The office manager at that time, Betty something...I can't remember her last name...took inventory of everything in the truck before it was offloaded into the warehouse. The painting was supposed to have been put into the big vault where it would be kept safe in a temperature and humidity controlled environment until the details of its purchase were complete and your parents were ready to deliver it..."

I frowned, remembering Pru's theory about my parents not knowing the painting was there. "They were expecting it?"

Dev narrowed his gaze on me and didn't speak for a long moment. "Of course. Why else would the painting be in that truck?"

"Where were they supposed to deliver the painting?" Hal asked.

"Uh...some royal prince in Dubai I think. I wasn't

really involved much in that side of the business. But Brent had told me about it. About how rare and valuable it was. I remember telling him it was dangerous to have something so valuable in the warehouse but he wasn't worried." Dev frowned. "Your dad never worried about anything. He had this ridiculously sunny personality that didn't allow any negative influence to take hold. That was why he and I worked so well together. He supplied the positive influence. I tainted it with harsh reality." Dev gave a harsh bark of laughter, shaking his head. "Anyway, he said they'd be delivering the painting soon and not to worry about it. So I didn't. I had too much other stuff to do and I trusted his instincts, even if they sometimes were a bit too optimistic. He always seemed able to make things work out."

"But things didn't work out, did they?" Hal asked.

"No. They didn't. Betty called Brent the next day and told him the painting was missing from the safe."

"How did that happen?" I asked, surprised. I remembered my father talking incessantly about how break-in proof that safe was.

"I have no idea. I've been trying to figure that out for two years, since they were killed. Because I know there's a direct connection between the missing painting and their deaths."

"You think whoever stole it killed them?"

Dev nodded. "I know it. But I'll be dammed if I can figure out who it is."

"Did the police ever figure out how it was stolen?"

"They think the Monet was swapped out for another piece of art. There was a cheap picture of cats that was almost exactly the same size as the Monet in the safe when Betty went to check her inventory. It was wrapped just like the Monet had been but it wasn't worth more than ten dollars."

"Someone knew the Monet was coming and was ready to swap it out."

"It sure looked that way to me."

"What did my dad think?" I asked.

"I never got a chance to talk to him about it. He was out of the office all that day and then he and Joline flew out that afternoon to make a couple of short hop deliveries. They died that night."

"What was he doing that afternoon?"

Uncle Dev looked at Hal. "That's what I've been trying to piece together. I figured he knew what happened to the painting and was trying to get it back. But we'll never know now because all the people who were involved are gone."

"Betty?" I said with a frown. I vaguely remembered a heavyset, middle-aged woman who used to give me a sucker whenever I'd come into the office. But I hadn't been in there for several years. I'd been too involved in my own life at that point.

In that moment I really wished I hadn't been.

"She died a couple of weeks later. Drove her car off the road. They assumed she'd had a heart attack behind the wheel."

"And the other people who worked there?" Hal asked.

"That was it. Me, Betty, Brent and Joline. It was a small, family operation. There was an auctioneer who came up from Kentucky a few times a year but that was it."

"Do you know how to contact the auctioneer?" Hal asked.

Dev frowned. "His contact info's probably in the office. But who knows if it's current. That was a couple of years ago."

I looked at Hal. "We can go over there tonight."

He nodded.

"What about me?" Devon asked. "I don't have any place else to go."

"What happened to all your money?" I asked him.

"What money? I've spent everything I had trying to lay low over the last two years. I've got nothing but my land and that rundown cabin."

I thought about it for a moment and made a decision. "You can stay here for now. We'll figure out what to do with you after we've put all this behind us."

Devon nodded. "Thanks, honey."

I held up a hand. "Don't! We're not okay, you and I. You're not my Uncle Dev any more. Right now, you're just a guy who only cares about taking care of himself."

He hung his head. "I guess I deserve that."

"And so much more," Hal said softly.

"I'll make it up to you, Joey. I promise."

"I don't want your promises. I want you to step up and help us fix this mess. Until I see that you've decided to man up, you're dead to me."

I wish I could say telling him off made me feel better. But it didn't. The truth was that Uncle Dev, for all his faults, was my last connection to the two people I'd loved more than anything in the world.

And pushing him away was like ripping another piece of their memory out by the roots.

CHAPTER EIGHTEEN

Fortunately, the rain had stopped by the time we pulled up to *Fulle-Proof Auctions*. The gates were chained and padlocked, a circumstance I hadn't considered when we left the house. I stared at the lock for a long moment, silently kicking myself for not remembering about the gate. "Do you know where there's a key?" Hal asked me.

"No. My parents always kept a key with them but I have no idea where it ended up after they died. I haven't..." I sighed, suddenly overcome with weariness and guilt. "This is the first time I've been here since."

"Who's been running the business?" Hal asked gently.

"Nobody. It's been on hold. For a while after the funeral people continued to contact me. But when I didn't return any of their calls they eventually stopped calling."

He didn't say anything for a moment. Then he walked back to the SUV and, for a beat, I thought he was going to climb inside and drive back to the house.

But instead, he opened the hatch in the back and reached inside, extracting something I couldn't see.

My eyes widened when I saw the bolt cutters in his hands. He shrugged. "They come in handy more often than you'd think."

I held up a hand. "I don't want to know."

It took only a second for Hal to clip the shank of the old padlock. I was suddenly not surprised the Monet had gone missing from the warehouse. My parents' idea of security was lacking, despite the eight-foot-tall chain-link fence surrounding the yard.

We climbed back into the SUV and Hal drove to the office building. It was a small, brick ranch that had once been a farmhouse. The business owned a hundred acres all around the home and in its heyday, it had used almost every square foot of that space for something.

I used the office key I'd retrieved from my father's desk at home and opened the door. Hal pulled his gun, motioning for me to wait outside. A moment later he reappeared in the doorway. "It's clear."

The outer office smelled musty, unused. I flicked the light switch and was instantly transported back several years, to the happy times I'd spent playing and doing homework in that very room.

My memories took me beyond the thick layer of

dust and the feeling of quick abandonment overlaying the space. Betty's desk was covered in folders, some open and some stacked neatly on one corner. A tea mug sat on her ugly green blotter, the white interior stained by years of use. A thin, pink cardigan still hung on the back of her chair and I suddenly knew there'd be a pair of knit slippers with hard soles beneath the desk. Betty's family might have been one of the calls I didn't take in the days after the funeral. They would probably like to get hold of her personal effects.

I added that task to my growing list of to-dos.

"Where would the personnel records be?" Hal asked, yanking me from my reverie.

I looked toward my mother's office door. "My mom kept them in a folder in her desk drawer."

He waited for me to lead the way. I dug deep for the strength to finally meet my fear head-on and opened her door.

I'd expected the sweet scent of violets to assail me when I walked into the tiny office. There might have been a tinge of it beneath the sour scent of being too long closed up, but it was as if she'd been expunged from the room.

There were no personal effects in the office, except for one photo of me as a baby on her desk and one of all three of us in a rowboat on Lake Everett when I was about five. I stood in front of that picture, feeling a smile tugging on my lips as I remembered the day.

It had been sunny and so hot, although it was still very early in the day when the man on the dock snapped our picture.

My gaze caught on two small boxes stacked next to the desk. I figured those contained my mother's things. Apparently, Betty had started the process of cleaning out the office after they'd died. And before she'd followed them into the ether herself.

"Here it is. Michael Blount. Does that name ring a bell?"

I turned away from my memories and nodded. "Yes. That's the auctioneer. As I remember he was pretty old the last time I saw him so he's probably retired by now."

Hal jotted the information onto a small slip of paper and handed it to me. I shoved it into the pocket of my jeans.

I looked around the room, feeling surprisingly removed from everything there. Hal pulled the file drawer open on her desk and finger-walked through the files.

"What are you looking for?"

"A client list. Maybe that will tell us where the painting came from."

"I'll check my dad's office. I think he kept the inventory sheets there."

Hal continued to search through my mom's things as I left the room. My father's office was next door to mom's, in what would have been a bedroom before the house was turned into an office. It was slightly smaller than my mother's but, where she had a view out over the grass at the front, his looked out on the lot. A much less pleasant but more practical view for overseeing the business.

Unlike my mother's office, my dad's office still held faint traces of him. It smelled of the cigars he used to love and the bookshelves between the room's two windows were covered in personal things. There were ratty old baseball caps, soccer trophies from my high school days, and lots of other things that invited me to linger and remember. But it wasn't the time for memories. I would come back, I decided. It was long past time the ghosts of that past were laid to rest.

I moved over to the metal file cabinet and pulled open the first drawer, going very still with shock as I looked inside. I pulled the other three drawers open and stood back, icy fingers of fear gliding up my spine. "Hal!"

He came into the room a moment later, the personnel file and a couple of others clutched in one hand. "Did you find something?"

I jerked my chin toward the cabinet. "That's where Dad kept the inventory files."

He walked over and looked down into the empty drawers, then slowly lifted his gaze to mine.

I don't know if my PI got any sleep that night. I was relieved when we got home to see that Pru Frect was gone. But later, as I lay in my bed with my mind racing, unable to sleep, I recognized that I was being selfish.

Without her help, Hal was on his own protecting me. He'd positioned himself on the couch downstairs with his gun near at hand. And I was pretty sure he would have loved some backup so he could get at least a couple of hours of sleep.

I'd given him Caphy, so at least he'd have some advance warning if someone tried to get into the house.

At three AM I gave up trying to sleep and crawled out of bed. I crept downstairs and into the living room, finding Hal sitting upright, his eyes closed and his gun clutched in his hand.

Caphy's head jerked up and her tail slapped against the floor a couple of times when she saw me.

Hal's eyes snapped open.

"It's just me," I told him quietly. "I couldn't sleep."

He scrubbed a hand over his face. "Okay."

Guilt ate at me. "Can I get you anything?"

"No. I'm good."

I sat down next to him on the couch, curling up in one corner. Caphy jumped up and circled between us, then finally landed with her head on my leg, sighing expansively before dropping back to sleep.

"I'm sorry about before."

He shrugged. "I get it. This has opened a lot of wounds."

"Yeah."

We sat in silence for a minute and then I said. "I haven't spoken to Uncle Dev for almost two years. I can't believe he's been in hiding almost all that time."

"Clearly somebody thinks he knows something about the painting."

"Do you think he does?"

"I think he knows something he's not telling us. He's protecting somebody."

"Or something." I chewed on my bottom lip.

"Do you think he's the one who emptied the file cabinet in your dad's office?"

I thought about that for a moment and then shrugged. "If he's mixed up in the theft of that painting then he's the obvious choice. Somebody didn't want us to find out who arranged for that painting to be here."

"I agree that seems to be the obvious conclusion."

I looked up. "But why take all the files?"

"They couldn't risk that you or somebody, maybe Dev, would figure out which file was missing."

"That makes sense." I sighed, my fingers digging through Caphy's fur in a soothing rhythm.

Hal didn't speak for a long moment and I glanced his way. His eyes were closed and his body had gone soft.

He was asleep.

I smiled. I'd let him sleep the last couple of hours until morning. Caphy and I would keep watch for a while.

A long, whistling snore filled the space between us and I chuckled as Caphy rolled onto her back, all four sticks poking the air above her thick body, and let loose another snore. Scratch that. I would keep watch. My two fearless watchdogs were currently too busy sawing logs.

But I was determined not to waste the time. I put it to good use considering what we'd learned so far.

We'd found Michael Blount's contact info in the personnel folder and planned to contact him in the morning. We knew where Uncle Dev was, and I wasn't done pestering him for answers. We knew who the mysterious body in the chipper was. I blinked, having a face/palm moment when I remembered we hadn't called Arno to tell him what we'd learned.

Unfortunately, if we did that, I'd have to tell my friend the cop where we'd gotten the information.

I sighed. Did I owe it to Dev to keep his secret? I just wasn't sure. I decided to pay him another visit in the hanger the next day, after our visit to Heather Masterson in the morning. Frowning at the thought, I briefly considered bowing out of the visit. Hal and I had so much to do. We could contact the artist by phone to ask her if she'd seen or heard anything on the morning of the murder.

But then I remembered how excited Hal had seemed at the prospect of meeting the artist and I decided against canceling. He'd given up enough for me. He deserved a little fun.

Hal's Pru-fect FBI friend was hopefully digging around on her end trying to find out if anybody knew who'd sent the painting to *Fulle-Proof Auctions*.

And we still had Buck Mitzner to consider. We hadn't made it out to his house because of the attack on *Country Road 57*. Was it possible, as Hal suspected, that Reverend Smythe was lying to protect Buck? I didn't believe it. But I recognized that I couldn't be entirely unbiased with the people I'd known for years, so I was inclined to trust his judgment on that.

But how did I figure out what was true and what wasn't? I had a sudden inspiration and filed it away to examine later. Maybe there was more than one way to skin a cat.

Gawd! I hated that expression.

Through the Caphy-smudged glass of the big window across the room, the sky was turning a stunning combination of orange and gold. The ball of light rose beyond the distant line of trees, giving it a magical aura. Morning was coming. And with it would come a new set of challenges. All of them seemingly impossible.

The thought made me tired.

And at some point, as the sun crept ever higher in the sky, I closed my eyes and slept.

CHAPTER NINETEEN

*L*is was staying at her mother's house while she was in town. The tiny brick home was where she'd grown up and it looked almost exactly as I remembered it. Lis' dad had died a few years earlier of a heart attack, and her mother had been living alone in the small house ever since.

Mrs. Villa had been totally devoted to Lis and her husband when we were growing up and I wasn't sure how she'd be managing on her own.

She was standing on the tiny porch when we drove up, a newspaper in one hand. Mrs. Villa smiled widely when she saw me, a pink flush staining her sculpted cheeks. "Joey! I'm so glad you and Lis connected. I told her I'd run into you at *Mitzner's* and she was anxious to see you again."

I couldn't help smiling back as the other woman swept me up into a hug. Like her daughter, Mrs. Villa was very tall for a woman. She towered over me as she scooped me into her long, toned arms and held me tight. "You look gorgeous as always," she told me as she held me at arm's length.

"So do you," I said. "I see where Lis gets her stunning looks." It was the truth. The slightly overweight, shy and unassuming woman I remembered had transformed into someone I barely recognized.

Mrs. Villa snorted out a laugh. "Stop it. You don't have to lie. I already love you."

Her clear blue gaze slid to Hal and widened slightly. "Hello again. I didn't get a chance to ask you before...are you Jo Jo's special friend?"

My cheeks heated and warning bells clanged in my brain. Fortunately, poor Hal was saved from responding by Lis' arrival.

"Mom, you make him sound like an invisible playmate." Lis pecked her mom on the cheek. "I'll be back in time for yoga. Don't start without me."

Mrs. Villa laughed. "Not a chance. You kids have fun."

As her mother retreated back into the house, Lis and I slapped a high five. "Just in the nick of time," Lis said laughing.

"We were heading for the condom question fast," I agreed.

Hal opened the back door for Lis. "Condom question?"

"Oh yeah," Lis said, sliding inside the SUV. "You don't know what you just escaped."

"Mrs. Villa was like a very sweet flower on the

wallpaper when we were growing up," I told him. "You barely noticed she was there, except for this warm, wonderful essence that kind of infused the space around her."

Lis nodded. "There was only one thing she never failed to insert herself into..."

We both grimaced. "Poor choice of words," Lis admitted. "Mom anointed herself the sex destroyer for all my friends and me."

I laughed. "It's true. If a boy and a girl even walked within ten feet of each other, Lis' mom would demand to know what their intentions were as pertains to the physical act."

Hal's disbelieving look turned to a chuckle. "You're pulling my leg."

"We're not!" Lis insisted.

"Besides, that would be against the rules," I joked. "We'd need a condom for that."

Lis and I dissolved into laughter that lasted until we were on the road heading toward Heather Masterson's home in the ridges above the park.

It felt good to revisit a happy time with my best friend. I'd missed having Lis around.

When we finally wound down, Hal asked, "So, where am I going?"

"Oh, sorry," Lis said. "Take the next right turn. Park Road winds around the outside of the state park. She apparently lives deep in the woods."

Lis wasn't kidding. As Hal wound his way along the picturesque road, it felt like we'd entered an enchanted wood. "This is gorgeous and slightly terrifying," I told my friends.

"It is," Lis agreed. She looked at the business card with directions crafted in tiny, manically neat print on the back. "5408 is the number."

"There it is." I pointed to a mailbox that was attached to what looked like a fifteen-foot totem pole with the numbers worked into the animals along its length.

"Wow, that's really something," Hal said.

"Very artsy-fartsy," Lis said, giving me a grin.

Heather's driveway seemed like it was two miles long. It was little more than a narrow gravel ribbon through the dense tree cover, winding and gradually climbing until the house finally came into view.

It was a long, low clapboard house painted pale gray with bright blue shutters and a deep front porch.

Roughhewn critters scampered around the front "yard", which was really only a small area with no trees. The ground was covered in rough mulch instead of grass and dotted with whimsical carvings of animals and an assortment of birdbaths and feeders.

The whole effect was charming and kind of crowded.

"This is fun," I told my friends.

"Very woodsy." Lis' pretty face was folded into a frown.

I was guessing she was worried about the portrait she was about to sit for so I decided to tweak her a little. "Maybe she'll paint you as a wood nymph. You could pose naked hugging one of those little wooden bears."

Lis glared at me. "Har, Jo Jo. I have one word for you...splinters."

I winced. "Ergh. Scratch the naked part."

"You could wear a giant condom," Hal offered.

The front door swung open and a magical sprite stood looking at us, her small face a study in delight. The tiny creature clapped miniature, paint-covered fingers and danced happily on two petite and very bare feet. "You're here! Oh, I'm so happy." When she danced, the sparkly concoction she was draped in swung and danced with her, sparkling in the ray of sunshine that somehow found its way through all the trees to beam down on just the spot where she was standing.

"Come in, come in!" She clapped her hands again. "And you brought friends too. How wonderful!"

I shoved Lis forward, murmuring into her ear. "You go first. I think there might be a fashion model sized oven in there."

"Beware if she tries to fatten you up," Hal whispered.

Lis snorted out a laugh and followed the artist into the Hansel and Gretel house.

"Do you think she planned that sunlight thing?" I asked Hal.

He turned and looked up at an almost perfectly round open area in the trees, the golden ball of the sun filling it like a yolk in an egg ring. "Nah." He winked at me. "She's a forest sprite. It's magic."

"Come in, come in!" The sprite called out.

We stepped through the door and into the Twilight Zone.

The wood floor was covered with dozens of cotton rugs in varying sizes, shapes and colors. The wood itself was unfinished and looked to be of all different kinds and widths, with widely varying grain patterns. There didn't seem to be any rhyme or reason to the mix. It looked like a mashup of whatever the builder could lay his hands on.

"Isn't it beautiful?" the wood sprite asked.

I blinked, forcing a smile on my face that felt stiff and artificial. "Very...um..."

"What kinds of wood are here?" Hal asked. He crouched down and ran a hand over a wide plank with a more stripey grain.

"Oak, ash, pine, some mahogany I think." She looked around. "I think that's cherry over there by the stairs."

"It's not finished?" Hal asked, seeming truly interested.

"No. I'm totally ecofriendly. My woods are unfinished, protected only by some oil and these rugs. I use no chemicals in my home at all."

A spotted bug flew past my nose and I watched it land on the window over the kitchen sink. It joined what looked like hundreds of its beetle friends there. The insects sort of looked like ladybugs but the color on their backs was more pink than red. "No bug spray, I see." I tried to keep all judgment out of my tone, but I really didn't like the idea of bugs crawling all over my kitchen.

"None. I embrace all of Mother's creatures."

"Mother?" I looked around, wondering if the mother of the sprite would be a sprite too. Or maybe a fairy.

"Mother Nature." She looked at me as if I were of questionable worth. Clearly, eco was more than a goal for her. It was akin to a religion.

She pointed to the ceiling, which was open to the wood planks, the rafters visible. "I leave the ceiling open so the mouse poop can drop to the ground. That way I can just sweep it up."

I twitched, my gaze shooting to the floor to make sure I wasn't standing in a pile of the nasty stuff. "Oh. Really? How..."

"Very practical," Hal offered, his lips twitching.

She seemed to take that as a compliment. "Well," she turned to Lis, who'd gone pale during our strange conversation. "We really should get started."

Lis nodded. "Where do you want me?"

The artist pointed to an area at one end of the large room. There was a two-level log setup with a brown drape behind it. "You can change into your costume behind that screen over there. Then have a seat on that log chair."

Lis nodded, throwing me a wide-eyed glance as she went to do as she was told.

"Ms. Masterson, I've been a fan of your work for a long time."

She was mixing paints and preparing a canvas for her work. "Why thank you, Mr..." She frowned, turning to us. "Oh my, I've done it again. Please excuse me for not asking your names."

"I'm Hal Amity and this is Joey Fulle."

I gave her a little finger wave. "Hi."

"It's a pleasure to meet you both. I'm so glad you could come along. It will be fun to chat while I'm working."

"I'm sure Lis will have a lot of questions. She's never had her portrait done before."

"Oh, she won't be allowed to speak," Heather Masterson said, appalled. "I need her to remain perfectly still."

Lis emerged from behind the screen with her eyes wide. "Is this right?" she asked, dubiously.

She was dressed in a skin-tight one-piece outfit that stretched from her broad shoulders to her narrow hips. The stretchy fabric was flesh-colored with silvery sparkles, and was adorned by a ring of autumn colored leaves around her breasts and her hips. A matching ring of leaves encircled her head, the orange and red tones a great compliment to Lis' shiny auburn hair. But the pièce de résistance was the small, stuffed chipmunk perched on her left shoulder.

I snorted out a laugh and then coughed to cover it as the artist scanned me a look.

"That's perfect. Now take a seat on the lower level

and rest your elbows on the upper one." She hurried over and started fussing with Lis, moving her arms and legs and turning her head to an uncomfortable-looking position before she was satisfied. "Perfect. Now no moving. Don't talk or scratch or wiggle."

Lis frowned.

"I'll just grab some quick pictures..." Heather picked up an expensive-looking camera and snapped pictures of Lis in her leaf costume from all directions. "Okay. Now we can get started."

As Heather began slashing color across her canvas, Hal and I seated ourselves on a pair of chairs which were clearly crafted from rough lumber and sticks. The seats were hard and unpadded, but surprisingly comfortable.

"Where'd you get these chairs?" Hal asked, rubbing a hand over the smooth surface of one arm.

Heather kept working as she responded. "I made them. I made all of the furniture and built most of the house."

Hal's eyes went wide and I saw a new respect for the unconventional artist bloom there. "Really? By yourself?"

"Not entirely. But I did as much of it myself as I could. I thrive in nature, Hal..." Her hand stopped mid-stroke and she turned to him. "I may call you Hal?"

"Of course."

"Good. Please call me Heather." She went back to

work and I was shocked to see the seemingly random strokes of paint beginning to form a Lis-like shape on the canvas.

"That's amazing. You're very talented."

"Thank you, Hal. Working with wood soothes me."

"Did you cut the wood down from your own property?" I asked.

"I did." She frowned. "But I only used what I removed to make room for the house. I abhor excess cultivation. The woods are Mother's finest creation. They must be preserved at all costs."

I lifted my brows at Hal but he didn't bite.

"This is a beautiful area. It must be very inspiring to you," he said.

"You can't imagine. These woods and rivers and rocky ledges feed my soul, energize my work."

"Do you ever do any landscapes?" he asked.

Heather shook her head. "Not commercially. I prefer to paint people into nature. That's how I honor Mother's gifts."

Good grief, I thought uncharitably. I liked the woods as much as the next gal, but I didn't think it was healthy to center your entire existence around them.

But Hal was nodding with a thoughtful look on his handsome face. He seemed to be buying what the artist was selling. "It's a shame. With your centered view of nature you'd create beautiful art. You could take your place with some of the greatest artists. Like Monet, for example."

Ah! I finally saw where he was going with the line of questioning.

But Heather didn't seem affected by his suggestion. "We all must honor our gifts as we see fit. My talents don't lie in that area." She spared him a quick smile. "My work is unique, Hal. Lots of people do landscapes. But no one else paints people into artistic representations of nature. I'd rather be unique than famous."

I could respect her for that at least.

"Makes perfect sense." Hal returned her smile. "If you don't mind, we had a couple of quick questions for you about the other night...morning actually."

"Oh? What kinds of questions?"

"You heard about the murder on Joey's property?"

Heather's tiny hand stopped mid-stroke. She turned a horrified gaze on me. "Murder? Oh my god! How horrible for you? Was it someone you knew?"

"No. At least, I don't think so. The police haven't identified the victim yet," I told her. I watched the artist carefully, she seemed genuinely upset.

Heather dropped her head into her hand. "I can't believe such a horrible thing could happen here. *Deer Hollow* is a kind and loving place. Violence doesn't belong here." Her eyes sparkled with unshed tears.

"I agree," Hal said gently. "Which is why we need to get to the bottom of what happened. So we can make sure it doesn't happen again."

Heather sniffed. "Of course. How can I help?"

"Lori Pickering said you were sketching on the ridge near the road that morning. We were wondering if you'd seen or heard anything that might be helpful."

"Lori Pickering?" She shook her head.

"She works at the produce stand on *Country Road 57* near the turn-off to *Goat's Hollow Road*," I clarified.

"Ah. The pretty blonde woman." Heather nodded. "I'd like to capture her in snow and holly berries," she mused to herself. After a moment, she shook out of her thoughts. "She's correct. I was sketching the other morning. I often sketch the sunrise from that ridge. The colors rising up on the horizon there are stunning."

"Do you paint sunrises?" Hal asked.

"Paint, no. I sketch them. Someday I might put them to canvas. But I haven't exhausted my love of portraiture yet."

Apparently, Heather Masterson had a linear type personality. No artistic multi-tasking for her.

"What time did you arrive at the ledge?" Hal asked.

"I believe it was midnight."

"Midnight? That's very early to catch a sunrise."

"It is, yes. But I love the woods at night. I lie back and listen to the call of the night birds, the scream of the owls. She sighed, clearly deep in her happy place. I listen to the coyotes sing around their prey."

I twitched in surprise. Hearing the coyotes howl

and sing always made me sad. It was a reminder of how cruel nature was and I hated it. I understood that the coyotes needed to eat. Nature was built on survival of the strongest. But it still broke my heart. "You probably hear them a lot around here. You're not too far from the river. There are dozens of dens cut into the ridges there."

"Yes. Many dens," she agreed.

For long moments we sat in silence. I was shocked to see that Lis had been almost completely recreated on the canvas and, despite my doubts about the form the art would take, I had to admit the blossoming result was magical.

My friend looked like a beautiful fairy. Albeit one with alarmingly big feet.

"That's amazing," I told the artist.

She nodded, not bothering to pretend to humility.

"Did you hear or see anything that night?" Hal asked gently.

Heather didn't respond for a moment. Long enough that I thought she wasn't going to answer him, but then she nodded. "I did, actually. It was very distracting. I was trying to listen to the woods and I kept hearing the roar of some kind of engine."

"An ATV?" Hal suggested.

"You mean one of those all-terrain vehicles? It could have been. I hear them from time to time." She frowned. "The man who lives in the woods behind me has one. Sometimes he rides it through the park." She shook her head, clearly disgusted.

I had to assume that someone who was as eco-friendly as Heather Masterson would resent a gas-guzzling, noisy and stinky vehicle marring her ideal natural world.

"Did you by any chance see the vehicle on the road?" Hal asked.

"There was a truck. A big black one with a round insignia on the doors. It had something in the back. I guess it could have been one of those noisy machines."

"Did you recognize the symbol?"

"It was really dark as you can imagine. But I remember thinking it was familiar. And I'll admit I was curious what the truck was doing on the road so early."

"What time was that?"

"I think it was about two in the morning. I'd been on the ledge for a while at that point."

"You say it seemed familiar," Hal urged. "If you had to guess, what do you think the insignia represented?"

She barely hesitated. "That landscape place on the other end of town."

My pulse spiked and I leaned forward in my chair. "*Mitzner's?*"

"That's the place, yes. I protested there once about ten years ago. They were selling those cut Christmas trees." She glared down at her canvas, clearly still angry at the memory. "That's murder pure and simple," she finished. "I don't like murder and I really hate murderers." She glanced over at us. "That man, Mr. Mitzner, I often see him driving around with one of those chippers. In fact, I'm pretty sure he was using one not too long ago. I could hear it tearing helpless trees into pieces through the woods."

She dropped her paintbrush into a jar of liquid and stood up. "You've destroyed my mood. I need to go meditate before I can go on." Without another word she turned and left through a pair of unfinished French doors, descending a set of stairs to the floor of the woods beyond the glass.

I hurried over and looked out the door, just in time to see her drop into a cross-legged position on the ground.

"Can I move now?" Lis asked, barely moving her lips.

"You might as well, she's out there communing with nature," I told my friend.

Lis groaned, rotating her head back and forth as she stood up. "What a wackadoodle."

Hal was staring out the window, a thoughtful frown on his face.

"What's wrong?" I asked him.

He shook his head. "Nothing. I'm just thinking about what she told us." He turned his head and refocused on me. "I don't think we can ignore it any longer, Joey. Buck Mitzner's name just keeps popping up. We need to find out if he also has an ATV."

"Almost everybody has one of those around here," Lis offered.

"But not everybody was on the road at two am that day. And not everybody has a chipper on their property."

"And not everybody has serious anger issues," I couldn't help adding.

"I guess we know where we need to go next," Hal said.

I nodded, sighing my regret.

"To lunch?" Lis offered helpfully. "I'm starving and..." she glanced around the strange house, clearly searching for something. "I really need to pee."

CHAPTER TWENTY

$\mathcal{M}$y phone rang as we were climbing back into Hal's car a couple of hours later. I looked at the ID on the screen and grimaced. "Hey, Arno."

"Joey. Is there something you want to tell me?"

Where do I start? I asked myself. "I don't think so. Is there something you *want* me to tell you?"

Silence pulsed through the phone line. I waited patiently for him to elaborate. I got that he was mad. He was mostly always mad so I was used to that. But of all the things I'd done over the last couple of days, there wasn't a single one I wanted to share with him.

No sense making him even more mad.

"Buck Mitzner tells me you and that PI of yours have been harassing him and going behind his back to speak to Reverend Smythe about him."

I rolled my eyes over to Hal and he looked a question at me. I shook my head. "If asking him a couple of questions is harassing then I guess we did. But it wasn't my fault Reverend Smythe came over to my table at *Sonny's*. That was his idea."

More silence. Then, "Why did you speak to the Reverend about Buck?"

"More like he spoke to me. What exactly are you mad about, Arno?"

"I'm mad because I told you to stay out of this. From what I can tell you're doing the exact opposite of staying out. Do you know what the exact opposite of staying out is, Joey?"

"Um, staying in?"

"Yeah. *In* up to your delicate blonde eyebrows. We're dealin' with a killer here, Joey. This isn't a game."

That comment didn't sit well with me. "I know it's not a dang game, Arno. If you'll recall that body turned up on *my* property. Not *your* property. Not *Buck's* property. *My* property. Nobody has a bigger stake in this than me."

"I understand..."

"No. I don't think you do understand. I have a professional working with me. We're working this methodically. I know the stakes. But, whatever's going on, it's tied to my parents and their death and I have every intention of figuring it out."

"Not if you're in jail."

My pulse spiked and for the first time I understood just how mad he was. "You wouldn't do that."

"Try me."

"I haven't done anything illegal."

"Doesn't matter. I can hold you for twenty-four hours."

"Arno..."

"All I want is for you to keep me apprised. Like it or not, this is my job. Not yours. And I want to know why you believe it's tied to your parents."

I swung my gaze toward Hal again, thinking. Finally, I nodded, then realized he couldn't see me nod. "All right. We'll come in. We should be there in ten."

"I'll be holding my breath in anticipation."

Smartass.

~

*A*rno was waiting for us inside the door. He glanced toward the Information Officer at the front desk. "I'll take care of this, Bob."

Bob skimmed a heated look over Lis, whom I hadn't been able to convince to go back home, and then reluctantly nodded.

To my surprise, Arno took us through the small building, past half a dozen desks covered in paper and stained coffee mugs, and into a room marked with a small sign that said, *Interview*.

He wasn't fooling me. Interview was just a more polite word for *Interrogation*.

The room was hotter than Lis in front of a camera and smelled like stale coffee and sweat. The table in the center was heavy old wood, scarred and marked up from years of use, and with an iron ring bolted into the top.

I hoped Arno wasn't going to chain any of us up to that iron ring.

Though I wouldn't put it past him. Especially with the way he was eyeing my friend.

He inclined his head at her. "Lis. How's things?"

She shrugged, clearly fighting a grin. "Things are good, Arno. How's the crime biz?"

He shook his head. "Have a seat. This won't take long."

Hal waited for Lis and I to pull two of the four straight-backed wood chairs away from the table and drop into them before taking his own seat and crossing one long, muscular leg over the other at the knee. He fixed his dark green gaze on Arno and gave him cop face. Which I could tell bothered Arno because it was so unreadable.

I fought a smile. "What do you want to know," I asked Arno, glancing at my phone for the time just to annoy him. "We were just heading to *Sonny's* for lunch."

He held my gaze, his eyes narrowed, as he slowly pulled a small notebook across the table and grabbed a badly chewed pen, attempting to jot something down in the notebook. The pen didn't work so he pulled another one out of his pocket. That one didn't work either.

Finally, after Arno managed to waste a full minute

testing out some of the saddest looking pens I'd ever seen, Hal reached into an inside pocket of his jacket and extracted an expensive metal one, placing it very precisely in front of Arno.

Hal had donned the leather jacket before we came into the police station. Though I wondered why, I figured he had some kind of "guy" reason and didn't ask.

Arno stared at the pen for a beat, his jaw working, and then grasped it, giving Hal a tight smile. "Thanks."

Hal nodded and leaned back in his chair. It creaked ominously under his weight but he seemed unconcerned. He'd fixed his full attention on Arno.

But Arno was looking at me. "We figured out who the victim was," he said.

I leaned forward, clasping my hands on the table. "Really? Who was it?"

"He surely wasn't one of your parents' clients."

"How'd you ID him?" Hal asked, looking genuinely curious.

"Rashton found a small piece of skin with some ink on it. A very distinctive tattoo that we were able to use in identifying a homeless guy with a rap sheet who was mugged in Indianapolis several weeks ago."

When Hal frowned, I clarified. "Rashton Blessed owns the local funeral home. He's also the Coroner."

Hal nodded.

"And the blood in Devon Little's cabin is a match for our victim." Arno cocked his golden head, peering intensely at me. "Why do you think this man's murder is tied to your parents?"

I hesitated, not wanting to dredge their deaths back up again, and then decided there might be a way to give Arno what he needed without getting into the more personal details. "Cox told us the murder was a message for me."

"Agent Cox? Of the FBI?"

I nodded.

"What message?"

I ran a fingertip over a picture gouged into the table with the tip of a pen. It appeared to be a pair of lips with a tongue sticking out from between them. Not bad actually. Somebody was wasting his talent being a criminal. "He thinks the killer is searching for something that disappeared. Something that came through *Fulle-Proof Auctions* just before my parents died." I looked up, narrowing my gaze on Arno. "He thinks it's what got them killed."

"Your parents' death was an accident, Joey."

I just shrugged.

"Okay, I'll bite. What item was it?"

"A painting. A very valuable one."

"What the heck would a valuable painting be doing at the farm auction?"

"You knew my parents had a secondary business, overseeing private negotiations and sometimes making deliveries of those items for the interested parties?"

"I'd heard something like that."

"We believe that's what the painting was doing there. They were hired to serve as the intermediaries for the sale."

"By who?"

"I wish I knew. Those files were missing from the office."

Arno frowned. "Then it's probably just a tale Cox made up."

"I don't think you understand, Arno. *All* the files were missing from the office at the auction."

Surprise flickered briefly through his gaze before he mastered it and forced an unconcerned look onto his face. "I'm sure Betty just boxed them up or something after your parents died."

I shook my head. "Doubtful. She apparently boxed up the stuff in my mom's office and the boxes were still sitting there. Why would she have taken the files out of the office?"

"Do you know how the office manager died?" Hal asked Arno.

I turned a surprised glance his way but he wasn't looking at me. His gaze was locked onto Arno's and something passed between them.

"Wasn't it an accident?" Lis asked. Everyone turned to her and she flushed. "I remember reading about it at the time and thinking what a horrible coincidence it was that she'd go so quickly after your parents died. She apparently drove off *Country Road 57* at one of the higher elevations."

Hal and I shared a look. I had no doubt he was thinking about our own close call on that road.

"What?" Arno asked.

Hal sat up straight in his chair, his square jaw going taut. "Joey and I were nearly run off that same road yesterday."

Arno gritted his teeth. "And you were going to tell me that, when?"

"We've been kind of busy, Arno. Besides, you lied to us about Buck reporting that chipper stolen."

Arno flushed. "I didn't lie. I just wasn't sure about the timing and I wasn't going to give you a reason to harass a private citizen on the basis of bad information."

Yeah, that was a partial lie too and we both knew it. Arno suddenly couldn't look me in the eye. He didn't want me involved and he'd apparently do anything to stop me.

"Well, Buck repaid you for that by lying to you. That chipper was never stolen. Well, actually, it was, but it was apparently at his house when it was taken. Not at *Mitzner's*."

Arno's gaze went wide before he mastered it. "Where'd you hear that?"

"From the angry man himself."

Arno's square jaw tightened. "Tell me what happened on *CR57*."

Hal took him through the attack, describing the car and the exact location.

"Did you get a license plate number?"

209

"No. We were too busy trying to stay alive," I told him angrily.

He scrubbed a hand over his face. "Okay, what else aren't you telling me?"

I deliberately kept my gaze from Hal's. If I looked at him Arno might see the guilt in my expression. But there was no way I was going to tell him about Dev. Not until I was sure which side he was on.

He still had the potential to help us figure out what was going on. But not if he was in jail.

"Joey?"

I sighed. "Somebody came to my house and threatened me the other night."

"Threatened you? How?"

"There was somebody in the yard and Hal and Caphy went to check it out. Whoever it was grabbed me from behind and demanded that I tell him where the painting was."

Lis went pale. "Yikes! Joey, did he hurt you?"

My hand went to my throat before I could stop it and the softly growled words played through my mind. *Tell me or you'll die.*

I shook my head. "No. It just scared me."

Arno sat back in his chair, looking almost annoyed at my admission. Finally, he sighed. "Okay, it's looking like you two were right. Whatever's going on, it must be tied to you somehow."

Relief made me start to smile.

"But that's all the more reason to stay as far away

from it as possible. Maybe this would be a good time to go stay with Felicity in Indianapolis for a while."

"I'm not running away from this. I need to find out who's threatening me and stop it." What I really meant, and couldn't explain to Arno, was that I needed to find out why my parents really died.

"Joey..."

"Nope. I'm not leaving, Arno. You might as well give it up."

He looked at Hal as if hoping my PI could talk some sense into me. Hal just stared back at him. "If anything happens to her, Amity..."

"I won't let her get hurt," Hal told Arno.

Arno didn't look like he believed him but he let it drop. "I want to know why you keep harassing Buck Mitzner."

"It was his chipper, which, need I remind you, he'd had at his home not too far from the spot where it ended up with a dead guy in it. He lied to us about where it was. And his truck was spotted in the area early that morning."

Arno blinked. "Spotted? By who?"

"Heather Masterson."

"The artist?" He snorted. "That woman's a dingbat."

"Maybe," I told him. "But Lori Pickering saw her in the woods, sketching that morning so we spoke to her in case she'd seen or heard something. Turns out she heard an ATV and saw a truck with the *Mitzner's* logo on it driving back down the road."

"She identified Mitzner's truck?"

"Close enough. She saw a logo that she thought was from the landscaping company. It was dark."

Arno didn't look happy with the news. "Buck has an alibi."

"So Reverend Smythe tells me." I let that hang between us for a few minutes, hoping Arno would take the bait.

He didn't. "I'm not going to second guess the Rev. If he said Buck was with him then Buck was with him."

"You won't even take a look at Buck's truck? Just in case," I asked.

Arno glowered at me. I took that as a No.

"Does Buck have an ATV?" I asked him, lifting a brow.

Arno tried to hold my gaze but couldn't. He glanced away.

I would take that as a Yes.

"What about the auctioneer?" Hal asked.

Everybody looked his way. I frowned, not following him.

"Everyone else in the business died within days of each other. If it's tied to the auction and that missing painting, then he could have been targeted too."

Arno looked at me. "Have you followed up with him?"

"Not yet. We just got his information."

Arno stood up, holding his hand out. "Give it to me."

I dug through my pocket and came up with the slip of paper Hal had given me. I was glad I'd stuffed the number into my pocket to follow up on later.

Arno disappeared without another word and I looked at Lis. She widened her eyes at me. "He hasn't changed."

"Not even a little bit," I agreed.

"He's a good cop," Hal said.

We both looked at him and he shrugged. "He's intense. But that's what makes him good at his job."

The door opened and Arno came back inside, a worried frown on his handsome face.

"He's dead, isn't he?" I asked.

Arno dropped back into his chair. "Yeah. He supposedly fell down the stairs at his home."

We all sat in silence for a couple of minutes, sucking it in.

Finally, Arno broke the silence. "I don't think we can ignore the possibility that our recent murder and...events...are tied to your parents' death anymore, Joey."

"Well, duh!" I told him.

His frown deepened. "You sure you won't go to Indianapolis? Or to a beach somewhere far, far away?"

I stood up. "Nope. But I will try to let you know if I find anything else out."

"You'd better do more than try. It sounds like somebody's put you in their crosshairs and you won't be safe until they get what they're looking for. If then."

~

"*L*unch?" I asked as we exited the station.

"I think I lost my appetite," Lis said. "Maybe you should come to Guadalajara with me. Hal can keep digging here." Her voice was hopeful and I hated to disappoint but there was no way I was leaving my mess for Hal to clean up. "How about we go back to my place and have a beer or three."

Lis made a face. "I'd love to but I really shouldn't. It will bloat me for my shoot tomorrow. Can you just drop me off at home?"

"Sure."

I hugged Lis when we got to her house. She squeezed me extra tight. "Are you sure you don't want to come with me to Mexico? It'd be fun and nobody would be trying to kill you."

I chuckled. "I can't. I finally have a chance to find out what happened to my parents. I'm determined to see this through to the end. However it turns out." I tried to keep the worry off my face.

Lis sighed. "Okay. But be extra careful, okay? I don't want to lose my BFF."

"You got it."

I climbed back into Hal's car. "Home, James."

He gave me a crooked grin. "James must be the name of your *other* private investigator."

I shook my head. "Okay, home Hal."

"You don't have to be so formal. You can just call me Hal."

"Har."

We drove out of *Deer Hollow* and hit *Country Road 57*. I was relaxed, feeling as if we were finally making some progress and relieved that I no longer had to feel guilty about keeping stuff from Arno...mostly. Then I remembered the last time we'd been on *CR57*. Just like that, I tensed up. My gaze locked on the rear-view mirror, I watched for cars that had noses like a shark. Fortunately, there was nothing behind us but a truck.

A black truck.

My pulse spiked. "Hal."

He glanced in the mirror. "I know. I saw it."

He sped up, keeping the SUV just on the edge of what was safe for the curvy, dangerous road.

The truck moved ever closer, as if it had sped up too.

"That's got to be Buck."

Hal didn't respond. When I glanced his way I saw the tightness in his handsome face and the stiff way he held himself.

I wasn't the only one who was tense.

The truck eased up behind us, getting way too close to our bumper and weaving toward the other lane as if it was going to try to pull alongside.

The road took a sharp turn and the truck moved back, hugging our bumper as if we were connected.

SAM CHEEVER

My heart thumping against my ribs, I pulled out my cell phone. "I'm going to call Arno."

Hal nodded.

We took the curve too fast and the SUV's over-sized tires squealed in protest. Hal managed to just keep it under control. We were weaving dangerously as we hit the final straightaway before our turn onto my road.

The truck eased closer.

All I could see was the shape of someone wearing a ball cap behind the wheel. The sun glared across the surface of the mirror, making a positive ID impossible.

The phone rang several times. "Come on, Arno." My gaze was locked on the mirror and the black truck revved its big engine, surging toward our bumper and causing me to grab the dash. "He's going to hit us!"

Hal slammed his foot down on the gas pedal, swerving into the other lane in an effort to avoid impact.

Fear was a sour taste in my mouth. My heart pounded against my ribs and I nearly dropped the phone because my palms were so sweaty.

To my vast relief, Arno finally picked up the phone. "What is it Joey?"

"We're being chased by a black pickup truck. I think it's Buck."

"No, it's not. I'm standing next to Buck right now and his truck is parked behind us on the lot."

216

I looked at Hal, shaking my head. "Well, it's a black truck and it's been menacing us for a couple of miles now. After last time..."

"Okay, I'll send a unit. How close are you to your place?"

"A quarter-mile."

Hal punched the gas and we surged forward, barely slowing as the turn flew up on us.

He took the turn onto *Goat's Hollow Road* on two wheels, skidding sideways on the gravel as the truck blasted its horn and roared past.

I collapsed with relief, unable to speak as Hal eased the SUV to a stop and sat back, breathing hard.

It had just been a punk. A bad case of road rage.

I'd been sure we were about to die.

Arno's voice thumped in my ear, strident and filled with concern. "Joey! Talk to me!"

I pulled air into my lungs and forced myself to respond. "Sorry. False alarm. Just some jerk with road rage."

Arno's breathing changed like he was walking, and I could hear his boots crunching across gravel. He sighed. "Okay, well here's some news for you. The truck is clean."

I frowned. "Clean? Why do I care..." Then I comprehended what he was telling me. "But we don't care if Buck's fingerprints are in it. He owns the truck. They would be there."

"No, you don't understand. Completely clean. No prints at all except for a few on the door handle and steering wheel from Buck's driving it to town this morning."

Hal looked at me. "Buck's truck was wiped down," I told him.

He made the turn into my property with cop face.

"Okay, that's suspicious, right? He probably had to clean up all the blood from chipping up that poor guy."

"Let's not get ahead of ourselves." Arno didn't sound happy. "And there was mud all over the bed so I asked him what he'd been hauling. He said he hadn't hauled anything since getting the truck washed last week."

"He's lying, Arno."

"We don't know that. But I did ask him if he has an ATV..."

"He does. Doesn't he?"

"Yeah. But that doesn't mean anything, Joey. Everybody..."

"I know. Everybody has one. But guess what, Arno, I don't. And I can name at least five other people I know who don't have one. And none of them are on our suspect list."

CHAPTER TWENTY-ONE

*H*al left the car in the circular drive and we wobbled up the stairs. I didn't know about him, but I felt as if I'd fought a few rounds with an MMA champion. I opened the front door and Caphy jumped all over us, whining softly as she licked my face.

"Hey, girl." I hugged her tight. "Go on, do your business."

She lunged through the door, happy to be told to go out into the sunshine, where bugs danced through her death radar and birds and squirrels were forced to run for their lives.

"Beer," I told Hal, dropping my purse onto the table beside the door. "Just leave the door open for Caphy."

He nodded.

I'd expected him to argue with me about drinking

beer at one in the afternoon but he didn't. A clear indication that he was as wobbly as I was.

"I may never drive on that road again," I told him as we made our way to the kitchen.

"I'm wondering how long it would take me to get back to Indy on an ATV."

I laughed at the image. As I entered the kitchen my laugh died on my lips and I stopped breathing.

A man was perched on a tall stool at my island, his gaze locked unflinchingly on us as we dragged to a surprised stop. "Hey, Joey."

Hal yanked his gun free and pointed it at my intruder.

I frowned. "How did you get in here?"

Devon Little shrugged. "You never changed the locks."

I would have to fix that right away. "You have no right..."

He held up a hand. "Before you launch into full lecture mode, I'm here for a very good reason."

"I can't imagine what would be a good enough reason for you to break into my home."

He reached down behind the stool and lifted something, placing it on top of my island.

I frowned. "Dad's painting?" Then I saw that he'd taken it out of the frame. "What did you do to it...?"

Devon shook his head. "Pipe down and come take a look." He reached over and tugged on the edge, pulling the canvas free and lifting it. I felt my eyes go wide. There was another painting underneath.

Hal beat me to the island. "I'm guessing that's the Monet?"

Devon nodded. "I wasn't the first one to de-frame this picture, Joey. The staples holding the Cessna painting over the other one were newish. There were only a couple on each side. This was clearly meant to be a temporary hiding spot."

My gaze slid over the beautiful piece of art beneath the Cessna painting. I reached a finger toward it, wanting badly to caress the strokes of paint. "It's stunning."

Devon nodded. "Do you understand what I'm telling you?"

I blinked, forcing my gaze from the Monet. "Yes. Someone hid the painting there. But who? And when?"

"I'm guessing it was your dad."

My head was shaking almost before he finished speaking. "Why would dad..."

"He found the painting," Hal said. "He knew who the thief was."

"And I'm guessing he threatened to go to the police," Dev added.

"That's why he was killed," I breathed. Suddenly the valuable art didn't seem quite so appealing. "But how?"

Devon shrugged. "We might never know. Maybe he saw the person stealing the painting. Maybe Betty did and told him."

My gaze shot to his. "You knew?"

221

"That Betty was the killer's third victim? Yes. It was all just too handy. And Michael Blount too."

"The auctioneer," I breathed. "Arno checked on him and found out he was dead."

"Killed a couple of days after Betty. Though nobody realized it was murder. I drove out to his place after Betty died and discovered he was gone too. That was when I understood what we were dealing with."

"And when you became a recluse?" I suggested as the pieces fell together.

He nodded. "I thought it was better to keep my distance from you. The killer seems willing to do whatever it takes to get this painting back. I didn't believe you were in any danger until that FBI guy turned up at my place. At that point, something changed."

"But what?" Hal asked him. "Why would the killer suddenly start killing again after two years?"

"Cox," I said. "From what Pru said he couldn't let it lie. And when he came down here the killer probably thought there was new information."

"Unfortunately, that makes sense," Hal said.

"Cox is definitely a problem. He's been snooping around my place for months."

"He approached you?" I asked, surprised. "If he thinks you have the painting why's he pestering me?"

"I haven't spoken to the man. Not since right after your parents passed. But he's been on my property several times, watching me from a distance. I'm assuming he's been watching you too, probably hoping one of us would lead him to the painting."

A cold chill crept down my spine. "Is that why you left your cabin?"

"Yeah. I figured it was only a matter of time before Cox led the killer my way. And I wasn't wrong, was I?"

Hal slipped his gun back into the holster in the small of his back. I'd forgotten he was holding it. "You're assuming the killer thought the homeless guy was you?"

Devon pointedly skimmed a look over his clothing. "Yeah. My disguise worked out well for me, but apparently not for him."

"What do you mean?" I was confused.

"The homeless guy. I think his name was Tom. He'd been hanging around because I gave him food once in a while and he slept in the shed at the back of my property. He'd been mugged in Indy apparently and wanted nothing to do with city streets. So, he jumped a train and rode it into the country, hopping off near *New Fredrickstown* and hoofing it until he landed here."

Hal glanced a question and I clarified. "It's a town about seven miles away from here, slightly bigger than *Deer Hollow*. They have three traffic lights, I think." We shared a grin.

"Anyway, looking at Tom gave me an idea. People don't see guys like him. They don't want to look too closely. So, I let my hair grow and wore baggier, rattier clothes."

"You made yourself look like a bum," I verified.

"Exactly. Unfortunately for Tom, I'm pretty sure he moved into my cabin after I left and probably started heading the opposite way. He was about my height and age and he might have looked a bit like me under all that hair." Devon shrugged. "We white, middle-aged guys all look alike." He gave me a grin that took me back to much happier times.

Hal nodded. "You think he might have bathed and dressed in your clothes..."

"I'm guessing. Yes." Devon frowned, pain flitting through his gaze. "I told him to leave. I said there was somebody after me and if he was nearby when they came he'd be in danger. But apparently he didn't listen."

"If that's true, then Cox is directly responsible for the death of that poor man," I said.

We stood in silence for a moment, each of us buried in our own thoughts. I finally moved over to the refrigerator and pulled out three beers, handing one to each of the men and drinking deeply from my own. The icy beverage was refreshing and helped ease the knot of tension in my back and neck from the day's events. "So, what do we do now?" I jerked my head toward the painting on the counter. "With that?"

Dev wouldn't meet my gaze so I looked at Hal. "Call Pru and have her come get it. The sooner that thing's out of here the sooner you'll both be safe again."

"What about the killer?" Dev asked. The expression on his face made it clear he didn't care much for Hal's idea.

"Arno's working on it. We'll give him everything we know and let him do his job. As long as the killer doesn't see a way to get the painting, he should be neutralized for the moment."

I liked Hal's reasoning. It made sense. "Okay. Do it. Call her. She can deal with Cox internally at the FBI. Hopefully he won't bother us anymore either."

Hal made his call and Pru promised she was on her way. "She should be here in a couple of hours," he told Dev and me.

"Good. Then I'm going to go take a hot shower. My neck and shoulders are killing me."

Hal nodded, his gaze resting speculatively on Devon. "I'll keep an eye on the painting."

Implied in his statement and the rigid stance of his large frame, was that he'd also be watching Devon, since he didn't seem to be completely on board with our plan.

Caphy's nails clacked across the tile of the foyer and moved in our direction. She came into the kitchen, wet and muddy up to her shoulders and wearing a wide, doggy grin.

"Oh, Caphy girl. Did you go in the pond again?"

Her tail smacked against Hal's jeans-clad thigh.

"Maybe you should take her into the shower with you," he joked.

"Ugh."

Devon stepped forward. "I'll take her out and hose her off for you."

"Thanks," I told him gratefully. "I'll be back shortly."

"Take your time," Hal told me. "You look beat."

I was. But I wouldn't be able to rest until the painting was out of my house and in the proper hands. And it occurred to me that I would finally be accomplishing what I believed my parents had been trying to do before they were killed.

It would be a good way to honor their memory and help me put the pain behind me. Clutching those comforting thoughts close, I headed upstairs with a considerably lighter step.

I took a really long, really hot shower and emerged feeling human again. The house was quiet. Almost too quiet. With a start I realized that Caphy had never come back inside. I'd left the bedroom door cracked and if she'd been in the house she would have come looking for me.

I dressed quickly and headed downstairs.

The house felt empty. Though I called out to Hal and Caphy, neither one responded and my spidey senses went on full alert.

I ran into the kitchen and the first thing I noticed was that the painting was gone. The second thing I saw was my sexy PI, draped over the floor between the island and the sink, a bloody lump on the back of his dark head.

"Oh my god, Hal!" I ran over and checked his breathing, relieved to discover he was still alive. I checked his pulse and found it beating strongly underneath my fingertips. "Thank god," I murmured to myself. I slapped Hal gently on the cheek. "Hal, wake up." I slapped him a few more times, each time a little harder. The last time I slapped him his head snapped sideways and smacked against the cabinet.

A big hand shot up and grabbed my wrist. "I've already been assaulted once," he said in a gruff, pain-filled voice.

"Sorry. I was trying to wake you up."

His eyes fluttered open and he groaned, covering them with his hand. "You almost knocked me back out."

I grinned sheepishly. "Can you sit up?"

He shoved at the floor and I helped him lift himself into a seated position, easing him back against the cabinet. "What happened?"

Hal gingerly touched the knot on his head, grimacing. "I was rinsing the beer bottles in the sink and somebody hit me on the back of the head."

I spied the amber glass bottle beneath the counter and reached for it. "I'm guessing with this..."

Hal grabbed my hand before I could touch it. "Fingerprints."

I flushed with embarrassment.

Hal slipped a finger inside the lip of the bottle

227

and lifted it. There was a smear of blood on the bottom of the beer bottle.

I looked around. "Where's Dev?"

Hal frowned. "He was still outside with the dog when..." His eyes went wide. "The painting?"

"Gone."

Hal swore softly. But I barely noticed. His mention of my dog brought a new sense of panic. "I have to find Caphy."

"She's not in the house?"

"No." He shoved off the floor with one hand and settled the beer bottle onto the counter. "Let's go find her."

In that moment I think I fell a little bit in love with Hal Amity. He'd been attacked and the painting he'd just promised to turn over to his friend at the FBI had gone missing again and all he wanted to do was help me find my dog. "She might be with Dev."

I considered whether she would have followed him back to the hangar and decided she might have. She'd done it in the past. But an even darker series of thoughts were shoving their way to the forefront in my brain.

What if the killer was there? What if he'd taken the painting and done something to Dev? And what if my dog had gotten caught in the crossfire? "If she's not outside the house I need to call Arno."

Hal didn't argue. Apparently, he'd considered the same possibility I had.

Caphy was nowhere to be seen in the grounds

around the house. She wasn't in the pond and when I went into the woods and called her she didn't come running.

"This is bad," I told Hal.

"Let's not assume the worst. Maybe she just followed Devon out back."

"She would have come. She'd have heard us whistling and calling." My stomach twisted painfully and I was finding it difficult to breathe. A dull, steady pain throbbed in my chest. "I have a really bad feeling about this."

Hal patted my back. "Call Arno. Then we'll head back to the hangar." His handsome face was tight with pain and something else. He looked worried. More worried even than Caphy's disappearance seemed to warrant. "What is it?"

He looked at the ground, avoiding my gaze. Cold slimy terror gripped my lungs. "Tell me, Hal."

"Whoever attacked me took my gun."

My knees buckled. And I thought for a beat that I might be sick. He grabbed my arm, tugging me upright as stars burst before my eyes. "She'll be okay, Joey. Don't poke your toes over the edge of the cliff."

I sucked air, panting with alarm. "What does that even mean?"

He actually smiled. "My mom used to tell me that all the time. It means don't come to the worst conclusion. Don't borrow trouble. However you want to say it. Let's keep it positive until we know something that makes that impossible."

I swallowed bile and scrubbed a shaky hand over my clammy forehead. "Okay, I'm positive I have a bad feeling about this."

He clapped me gently on the back. "That's my girl."

A small silver car pulled up my driveway and we turned to look, thinking that Pru had finally arrived.

"At least Pru'll have her gun," I said, raising my arm to let her know where we were.

Hal grabbed my arm and yanked it down. "That's not Pru." He pulled me backward, into the shade of the trees at the edge of the woods. "Head into the woods and call Arno."

I started to argue.

He tugged my arm none too gently. "Joey, do as I say. I promised Arno I'd keep you safe and that's what I intend to do."

I frowned.

"Circle around and go to the hangar. If you find Caphy take her into the office with you and lock yourself in. Wait there until Arno or I come to get you."

I didn't like the sound of that. "I'm not going to leave you alone."

"Joey, I don't have time to argue with you."

The little car stopped behind Hal's SUV and the door opened. A man climbed out. A man in a light gray suit.

"It's just Cox."

Hal grabbed my phone and hit 9-1-1 then he shoved it back at me. "Do as I said!"

A voice came on and I watched him stride out of the woods, toward the agent waiting for him on my circular drive.

"9-1-1. What is your emergency?"

"This is Joey Fulle out on *Goat's Hollow Road*. I need to report a theft and an attack..."

The operator asked me several questions. I only half listened as I watched Hal approach Cox and stop in front of the smaller man, his stance rigid with anger. One of Hal's hands kept moving backward, toward the gun that wasn't there. That, more than anything told me he didn't trust the other man.

"Miss Fulle?"

I forced my mind back to the call. "Yes. I'm sorry."

"Officers have been dispatched. I want you to promise me you'll stay on the phone until they get there."

To my horror, Cox reached into his jacket and came out with a gun, pointing it at Hal's broad, unprotected chest. I dropped the phone and started forward.

In the distance I heard a tiny voice calling my name. *Miss Fulle? Are you there? I need you to stay on the line...*

Hal's hands curved into fists. I stopped, unsure what to do. If I marched over there then Cox would just have two people at gunpoint and Hal wouldn't be even a tiny bit safer. But if I stayed where I was...

I thought about doing as Hal had said, but by the time I circled around and got to the hangar there was no telling what Cox would have done to him.

If I could get to the house... I eyed the clumps of large evergreens interspersed across the yard. I could use them to hide my progress across the yard. But there was a large open area between me and the first copse of trees.

I'd never make it before Cox saw me.

Then my worst nightmare happened and my decision was ripped out of my hands. Caphy ran from the back of the property, growling and barking with her tail in the high, fast wag that signaled maximum aggression. She turned the corner of the house and spotted Cox, then took off like a shot directly toward him, and Cox shifted his gun away from Hal, pointing it directly at my dog.

CHAPTER TWENTY-TWO

"No!" I screamed and took off running. At the very least maybe Cox would see me coming and get confused about who to shoot. Unfortunately, he knew who the greatest threat was. He kept the gun pointed at Caphy as she bounded ever closer, teeth bared.

"Caphy, no!" She didn't hear me, or wasn't able to redirect her obsessive focus on the man she'd correctly identified as a threat.

Hal turned when I screamed and finally realized what was about to happen. His gaze found mine and filled with fear.

"Hal! Help her! I screamed."

Hal spun and whipped his arm up, smashing it against Cox's arm. But it was too late.

The gun went off, sending death through the air, searching for my sweet, over-protective pitty, and Caphy yelped as the bullet found its mark.

I screamed long and wild as grief tore massive holes in my heart. My steps faltered as Caphy staggered backward, one leg lifted as she yelped with pain.

I threw myself in her direction, reaching her as she fell to her side in the dirt, panting and crying in pain.

I could barely see her through the tears. I dropped to my knees beside her and covered her with my body, kissing the soft, squishy width between her beautiful green eyes. She lay on her side, her broad chest heaving as shock took its toll on her compact, furry body.

She swept a broad, pink tongue over my face, a rough caress meant to soothe me even as she fought pain and fear of her own.

Sirens sounded in the distance shrieking ever closer as I lay sobbing over my dog. But in that moment I didn't care. I didn't care about Cox or the stupid painting or anything else except my dog.

Suddenly firm hands found me, wrenching me away from Caphy. I cried out, trying to grab hold of her again.

"Joey, let me have her. We need to get her to the vet."

I slapped at his hands, inconsolable and sobbing violently.

Hal tried to be gentle. He tried to soothe. And then he did the only thing he could.

"Dammit, Joey. Pull those toes back from the cliff. We have a pit bull to save!"

Like a bucket of cold water his words finally cut through my inconsolable grief. I jerked backward, nodding sharply, and let him get to Caphy. He carefully gathered her into his arms, rising from the ground with her pressed tightly against his chest. We ran toward his car.

Arno ran up to us as I was pulling the back door open so he could put her on the seat.

"What happened?"

"We'll tell you later. Just arrest that man over there," Hal said.

To his credit, Arno took one look at my dog and my devastated face and nodded. "Call me as soon as you can so I know what I'm doing with the *FBI agent*."

His emphasis on the title was no doubt meant to convey a message to my PI. I was too far gone to realize it at the time or to care. I slipped into the back seat and Hal draped my pibl gently across my lap.

Just before Hal closed the door I yelled out at Arno, "Call Doc Beetle."

Arno nodded and he was already talking on his cell as Hal slammed the car into gear and tore away from the house.

*D*oc was standing at the door when we arrived. He motioned for Hal to carry her into the exam room we'd visited the last time we'd brought my dog to the clinic. That time seemed like eons ago but it had only been a couple of days.

My poor pitty.

Doc quickly set to work as soon as Hal laid Caphy across the table. She offered a gentle little wag of her tail when Doc laid a gnarled old hand on her and gave her shoulder a scratch. "Now you and I are seeing entirely too much of each other pretty girl."

Caphy's tail smacked the stainless steel again and I barely contained a sob.

Doc looked at me. "Maybe you should wait outside."

I shook my head. "I'm staying."

He nodded, injecting something into Caphy's thigh. "Then make yourself useful. Go get that blanket I put into the dryer. We don't want our girl to get shocky."

I hurried to obey and, by the time I'd returned and draped the deliciously warm blanket over Caphy's shoulders, Doc already had the wound site shaved and was examining it.

"It's a clean shot. Through and through."

I wasn't entirely sure what that meant, but by the way Hal relaxed I thought it must be a good thing. "Okay."

Doc glanced up, giving me a tight smile. No major

arteries hit or bones broken. No organs damaged. The bullet went right through the muscle and out the other side. A few stitches, one of those lovely drains you hate so much, antibiotics and rest and our little girl's going to be just fine."

A ten-thousand-pound weight lifted off my chest and I stumbled backward, dropping into the nearest chair. "Thank you, God." Maybe I'd go back to church after all.

Hal gave me an encouraging smile. "Can we take her home?"

I liked the way he said "we" and "home" in the same sentence. It made me all warm inside.

But Doc put a chill into my warm spot. "I need to keep her here tonight. I'd like to give her some blood and make sure we keep her fluids up and ward off that shock. But hopefully she can come home tomorrow."

I could live with that. There was nobody I trusted more with my dog's life than Doc Beetle. Except for maybe Hal Amity.

"Where's Sally?" I asked the doc. His assistant was usually there helping him with things like warmed blankets and IVs.

"She's visiting her mother in Indianapolis. I'll call her and have her come back this afternoon. We'll take turns keeping an eye on this little girl."

I nodded, feeling like melty butter now that the terror had fled. "We should probably get back then,

Joey," Hal told me gently. "Arno's going to want to know what's going on."

I nodded wearily. The last thing I wanted to deal with was giving Arno a statement. But I let Hal lead me out of the vet's office, after giving Caphy a kiss on her chubby cheek, and sat like a zombie in the front seat as he drove us home.

When we got there, Hal took pity on me and called Arno himself, filling him in on everything. Including Devon and the missing painting.

I lay down on the couch and closed my eyes and, before I even knew what hit me, I had drifted off to sleep.

~

I awoke to the sound of the television and the warm scent of tomato sauce and cheese. I wrenched my eyes open to find that Hal had covered me with a blanket at some point and was sitting on the other end of the couch with a beer in one hand and a slice of pizza in the other.

"I guess the temple has fallen?"

He glanced my way, his brows lifting when he saw that I was awake. "Temple?"

I nodded toward the slice in his hand.

Hal grinned. "I plead extraordinary circumstances."

"Ah. And what exactly are those circumstances?"

"The pizza place was the first one listed in the restaurant app and I was starving."

I chuckled.

"Are you feeling okay?" He set the slice on a plate and wiped his hands on a paper napkin.

I shoved myself upright and tugged the blanket up to my chin, feeling chilled. "I'm good. I slept like the dead. I must have needed it."

Hal nodded. "I thought you might be hungry when you woke up."

I eyed the half-eaten large pizza. "Well, at least somebody was hungry."

He grinned. "I'd blame Caphy for some of that but..."

My smile slid away. "Have you heard anything?"

"Yep. Doc Beetle called and said she's awake and draped alongside him on the couch, licking all the lint off his pants."

I laughed. "That's my girl."

"Seriously though, he says she'll be fine. She's a lucky girl."

I sighed. "I thought for sure I was going to lose her."

Hal patted my foot.

I looked at him and felt tears burning my eyes. "You saved her life."

He shrugged, flushing. "I didn't do enough."

"If you hadn't hit his arm he would have killed her. I owe you everything for that."

"No, you don't. Truth is I'd have been only slightly

less devastated than you if anything happened to that dog. She's wormed herself right into my heart."

"She has a way of doing that."

We shared a smile.

I scooted over and grabbed a slice of pizza, taking a bite and chewing thoughtfully. When I'd swallowed, I looked up at him. "What happened with Cox? Before Caphy showed up. Was he threatening you with the gun?"

"He was demanding the painting. When I told him it was gone he didn't believe me." Hal shook his head. "He had a crazy look in his eyes."

"How'd he find out we had it? Surely Pru didn't tell him?"

"That was what I wanted to know. When I called Arno to tell him what happened, he said Cox was ranting like a lunatic. He apparently admitted to attacking Prudence when he found out she was going to come retrieve the painting without him and killing poor Tom the homeless guy."

I almost choked on my pizza. "Are you serious?"

"As a heart attack." Hal took a big bite of his pizza.

"But why?"

"Killing the man he thought was Devon was a desperate attempt to get information on the painting's location. Cox was obsessed with that painting. At first I think it was just a need to stamp 'Closed' on a case he felt he should have easily settled two years ago. He apparently has a pretty good close record and it stuck in his craw that the painting got away from him. But when he started to realize how rare and valuable that painting was, I really think he'd begun to think about taking it himself." Hal shook his head. "Cox admitted taking Mitzner's truck and ATV too. I guess Mitzner wasn't lying."

"And Arno's instincts were right about him." I sighed. "I'll never live that down."

"And he was the one who attacked you that night in the yard."

I swallowed hard at the thought, nodding.

"I spoke to Pru," Hal said.

"She's okay?" I felt slightly guilty for not asking that question sooner. But not all that guilty.

"A little banged up but she's fine. She's coming down here to take charge of Cox in the morning."

I nodded. "I'll bet slapping him in cuffs after what he did to her will feel good."

"That's a good bet."

We ate in silence for a moment. Then it finally hit me. "It's over?"

Hal nodded. "Cox hasn't copped to killing your parents and the others yet but...yeah...I'd say, except for one big detail, we're close to putting this to rest."

I frowned. "Dev and the painting."

"Dev and the painting."

"He's probably in Mexico by now."

"You know Pru will find him. She's a good agent."

I eyed him for a while, an ugly swirl of jealousy spiraling through my belly. "Is that all she is?"

"What do you mean?"

"I mean..." Heat flared in my cheeks and I wanted to hide under the blanket. Instead I took a deep breath and plowed ahead. "Are you and Pru dating?"

Hal stared at me a long moment and then cocked his head. "Why are you asking?"

I chewed my lip as my cheeks proceeded to catch fire. "No reason. Just curious."

He nodded. "Well, to answer your question, no. Pru and I have never dated."

"Would you like to?" I couldn't believe the words fell out of my mouth. I should have had Doc Beetle stitch my renegade lips together before they got me into trouble.

"Not really. She's not my type." Hal moved closer, lifting my legs and placing them over his lap. "Would you like to know who *is* my type?"

Something warm and delicious swirled in my belly. Hal was flirting with me.

Before I could consider the full meaning of that thought, Hal leaned close and his lips were suddenly on mine. My world righted itself fully, bathed in the spicy taste of cheese and pizza sauce and infused with the delicious scent of a man who was sexier than should be legal.

It would have been the perfect moment.

For a beat in time it was.

But then an evil sprite inserted herself into the life-changing event and my world turned inside out again.

"Well isn't that sweet?"

Hal and I jerked apart, our heads whipping toward the door.

And we found ourselves looking at a cray-cray portrait artist holding a gun that was bigger than her head.

CHAPTER TWENTY-THREE

*H*eather Masterson sneered at us. "I hate to interrupt, but..."

Something told me she was lying. She didn't really hate to interrupt.

"How'd you get in here?" I asked an intruder for the second time that day. I really needed to get a new lock, or locks, on my front door.

She shrugged. "It wasn't locked."

Or just lock the one I had. *Oops.*

Hal eased away as I bent my legs to allow him to escape. Tucked as I was under a fleece blanket, I wasn't doing anything quickly. If I tried I'd most likely end up on the floor between the couch and the table, rolled up like a fleece burrito.

He lifted his hands. "You don't need that gun, Heather."

Her smile tightened. "I'll be the judge of what I need. Where's the painting?"

Uh oh. Not that again. Cox hadn't reacted well to the news that my negligent godparent had hoofed it with the stolen art. I had a feeling the woman who left her ceiling unfinished so mice could poop directly onto her unfinished wood floor wouldn't take it too well either.

I decided it was time for a little distraction. Maybe someone would rescue us if I stalled long enough. After all, it worked in the movies. "You're the one who killed the homeless guy?" Maybe Cox had been lying about his part in the murder. He was clearly unbalanced.

Cray-cray laughed, a high-pitched, slightly manic sound. "You think I stuffed a guy into a wood chipper? Please."

I eyed her diminutive form and realized she was right. Unless she was a sprite from a forest on Krypton, she probably hadn't lifted Tom the homeless guy into a chipper. "But you did kill my parents...?" Rage made me vibrate beneath the blankets.

"I did. They shouldn't have threatened me. If your father had just given me the painting they could have gone on about their business and no-one would have been the wiser."

"How'd he find out it was you?"

She frowned, going from uncaring to enraged in the beat of a heart. Cray-cray. "That old busybody told him. She saw me that day, on the lot. He put two and two together when the painting went missing."

"Betty?" Suddenly the pieces fell together. "And I'm assuming Michael Blount saw you too?"

"I'm not sure. I didn't think he had. But I needed to snip off all those loose ends. You know?" She grinned as if talking about murder was akin to planning a party.

"No. I don't know. Those people didn't do anything to you."

"I beg to differ, Missy. Your father took what was mine. He was going to tell the police I stole it."

I decided it wasn't a good idea to tell her the painting didn't belong to her. Yeah, I can be smart when I need to be. "How'd he get hold of it anyway?"

"I was meditating. He must have snuck into the house and grabbed it. Then he hid it and confronted me." Her diminutive face had gained several shades of red as she recalled the incident. The tiny hand that was wrapped around the enormous silver gun was shaking so hard the gun was wobbling.

I eyed that gun with trepidation. If her finger vibrated onto the trigger...

Hal must have shared my concern. "You need to put that gun down. There's no need to threaten us."

Heather shrugged. "I just want the painting. Give it to me and I'll go."

I wasn't a PI or a cop, but I was pretty sure that was a lie. Just like I understood that my parents had been doomed as soon as my dad approached the evil artist and told her what he knew. "We'll take you to it."

246

I could feel Hal go very still beside me and I prayed he wouldn't let on that I was stalling. I needn't have worried. My PI was intuitive and smart.

He nodded. "It's in Mr. Fulle's hangar."

I only hoped he could find a way to save us on the way to the hangar.

Heather flicked the gun toward the door. "Let's go then."

~

The sun was low on the horizon when we stepped outside. But the air was still hot enough to bring beads of sweat up on my brow as we made our way toward the back of the property. A blue heron rose silently out of the pond as we passed by and I watched it struggle to gain air beneath its massive wings, thinking as I always did that big birds had it rough. They worked so hard to get off the ground and they were in danger from predators until they managed to gain altitude.

I used to think the same thing about my dad's little Cessna. Though he'd explained the theory of aerodynamics to me several times as I was growing up.

Mostly because he liked to explain it. I didn't really care that much about the theories. Only the reality of the plane not plunging to the ground and taking my parents away from me.

I'd apparently always had a feeling the Cessna would be the way I'd lose them.

We followed a beaten-down path of tall grass toward the building, which sat quiet and unassuming in the growing dusk. My gaze slid hopefully toward the single, small window, hoping Uncle Dev was still there. Maybe the shock of seeing him would make Heather lose focus and give us a chance to tackle her and grab the gun.

I scanned Hal a look and he reached out to clasp my hand, giving it a squeeze.

I liked the warmth of his skin against mine and the feeling that I wasn't alone. So, I was happy when he didn't let me go. We reached the big doors to the hangar and stopped, looking at the woman with the gun.

"What are you waiting for? Open it."

"Sometimes wild animals nest in here," Hal told her with a straight face. "The building's been vacant for a long time."

I nodded enthusiastically. "My dog had a run-in with a skunk once. She was protecting her babies."

Hal gave my hand another squeeze. I assumed he liked my addition to his lie.

Heather eyed the doors, frowning. "Then I guess you're going in first. If anybody's going to get skunked it's going to be you two."

A strident cry sounded out beyond the runway, toward the not-too-distant line of trees separating our property from Uncle Dev's.

"Coyotes," I breathed, infusing the single word with as much terror as I could manufacture. The crazy artist liked to fancy herself a woman who understood nature, but I doubted she'd ever really interacted with the more dangerous denizens of Mother's world.

I held my breath as she stared off in the distance. Would she be spooked? Or just shake it off.

Her gaze slid to the doors and she waved her gun at them. "Let's get inside."

The shrill call sounded again and was quickly answered by several others.

Hal and I stared toward the woods and saw the shadows shifting there. A beat later a single, large gray coyote stepped from the trees and stood looking at us, its posture tense and hostile.

"Didn't you tell me this used to be a Native American burial ground?" Hal asked in a hushed voice.

I nodded, biting my lip and moving closer to him. "That's why there are so many coyotes around here. They were the tribe's spirit animal."

I skimmed Heather a quick look and saw her throat work over a hard swallow. Hal squeezed my hand again.

Two more coyotes stepped out of the woods and the long grass ruffled behind the artist. She lifted the gun and shot in that direction, her eyes wide with fear.

Hal took a step toward Heather but she whipped back around. "Don't move."

He raised his hands. "Not moving."

The grass shifted again, several feet from the first place she'd fired. Heather's arm whipped around and she fired two more times.

Hal pushed me behind him.

"Get those damn doors open," the artist yelled.

I scanned a look toward the tree line and saw a single figure standing where the coyotes had been. The man was bare-chested, with long, dark hair held back from his face by a brightly colored band around his temple. He wore a loincloth over leather chaps and held what looked like a bow in one hand.

I gasped, pointing toward the Native American figure and backing toward the building. "Oh my god, is that?"

Heather gave a small cry and lifted the gun again, her attention on the ghostly figure. Hal launched himself at her and they both went down, disappearing in the knee-length grass and weeds. The gun went off but the bullet pinged harmlessly away.

Sounds of scuffling ensued and I left Hal to it, thinking that if he couldn't best a ninety-pound woman then he was in the wrong business.

Even if she *was* crazy and had a gun.

I looked back toward the tree line and Uncle Dev waved before turning and disappearing into the trees.

I remembered that costume from Halloween when I was ten. I'd gone as a Native American too, but I'd been a princess. I smiled at the memory.

Hal dragged Heather Masterson out of the grass

and I saw that he'd cuffed her hands behind her back. I couldn't help wondering where he'd been hiding those cuffs...

Her small face was dark with rage and she was spewing just about every swear word I'd ever heard, and then some. She repeatedly tried to jerk out of Hal's grip but she wasn't going anywhere.

"Let's get *this* back to the house so I can call Arno."

Heather spit at him and he sidestepped it, shaking his head.

I nodded, then had a thought. "Wait, let me check something first?"

He nodded and I quickly opened the hangar doors, ducking inside. The office was pretty much the same way we'd left it. Except for the missing remote-control cars on the shelf.

But that was the only exception. To my pleasure, I saw that the Cessna painting was back in its frame and hanging on the wall where it had always hung.

I smiled.

Turning away, I left the office and returned to Hal and his literally spitting mad prisoner. "Okay, let's go."

He gave me a look but I shook my head and we took off toward home.

*A*rno sat across from us and jotted notes as we told him about our face-off with Heather Masterson. I left my uncle's participation out of the storytelling because, even though he'd clearly considered stealing the painting again, he hadn't ended up doing it.

My own beef with him about leaving me in the crosshairs of a crazy killer was private. I would deal with that later.

But for the moment...

The front door opened and the young uniformed deputy Arno had sent out to the hangar walked in with the Cessna painting under one arm. It was the quick work of only a couple of minutes to pull the frame off and tug the top canvas free.

Arno stepped back to admire the Monet, whistling softly. "I'd given up on ever finding this painting."

"I can't believe it was hanging in my father's office."

Arno glanced my way. "About that..."

"Stop thinking what you're thinking," I told him. "My dad only took it from her so he could return it to the right people."

"Then why didn't he?"

"He had a delivery that day. I'm guessing he was trying to figure out what to do with Heather Masterson. She's been a point of interest and a fixture in *Deer Hollow* for most of our lives. And she has powerful friends. He most likely wanted to consider his options carefully before he accused her."

Hal frowned, looking very unhappy, and I made a mental note to ask him why after Arno left.

"He shouldn't have made his delivery that day," Arno said.

I shrugged. "He was kind of anal about doing what he'd promised. But I agree. Hindsight says he should have stayed home and dealt with the more important problems of the stolen painting and Heather Masterson."

And his poor decision had ended up costing three more people their lives. A ball of pain danced in my belly with the thought. I wondered how long it would take me to view him again the way I had growing up. As a kind and talented man who'd always done his best for the people around him and the community that nurtured and supported us.

I gave a small sigh and Hal wrapped an arm around me.

"Just so you know, the car that menaced you?"

I nodded.

"Heather Masterson's car. She didn't drive it into town very often so it didn't occur to me at first. But when she became a person of interest I checked her home and found it. I also found some letters to her from Devon Little."

I felt my eyes go wide. "Uncle Dev? What were they about?"

Arno shrugged. "They're part of the investigation

now so I can't reveal their contents. But suffice it to say he was involved in getting that painting here. To *Deer Hollow*."

Hal stiffened beside me. "He was Cox's informant."

Arno just stared at my PI while I turned to a puddle of sloppy regret beside him. Had I let an accomplice to murder go? My gaze jerked to Arno's. "Did he have anything to do with killing my parents?"

"We won't know until we capture him." Arno glanced at Hal. "Thank you for giving us the heads up on his whereabouts."

Hal jerked his head in an uncomfortable nod while I did my best not to stare at him with my mouth open.

"Well, I'll get going. I have paperwork," Arno said. He fixed us with a speculative gaze but finally turned away and left.

As soon as the door closed behind him, I whirled on Hal. "You squealed?"

To his credit, he didn't flinch away. "Yes."

I was at a loss for how to respond to that naked admission. "I...you..." Then it hit me. He'd saved my butt again. I should have told Arno about Dev but hadn't. I'd fallen into my old role of protecting my family and it had put me on the wrong side of the law. I didn't like that he'd gone behind my back. But I understood it. "It was the right thing. I'm sorry I didn't do it myself, so you didn't have to."

Hal didn't say anything. He clearly hadn't been happy to do it either.

I dropped onto the couch, feeling too drained to even speak.

Hal took a seat next to me and we sat in silence for several moments. Finally, I turned to him. "I guess that explains why you look like you want to punch somebody."

"You mean like your Uncle?"

"Yeah, he deserves a good punching. But in the end, he did leave the painting and he helped us with Heather."

"How did he know we were going to need that help?" Hal asked, one dark eyebrow lifted.

I frowned. "You think he's still communicating with Heather." It wasn't a question.

"He double-crossed your parents all those years ago. Took advantage of their side business to make some money for himself. And I'm guessing he was the one who implicated your parents with the theft of the painting."

I thought about what he said and realized, with a painful jolt, that it made perfect sense. If he'd arranged for the stolen painting to come to *Deer Hollow*, and then told Cox it was there so he could point a finger at my parents with the FBI, then... I gasped. "Heather never saw who took the painting."

Hal nodded. "Devon probably told her it was your father. When your dad confronted her based on

Betty's information of having seen her hanging around the Auction that day, it just verified her suspicions."

I frowned. "But wouldn't he have been confused when she accused him of taking the painting?"

"Probably. But if your dad was as good on his feet as you are, I'm guessing he went along with her accusation and tried to leverage it."

His compliment gave me a warm spot until I made the next connection. "And it got them killed," I murmured, my heart breaking. "That means that even if Devon didn't put those rocks on the runway..."

"He signed their death warrants. And he hid the cause of their deaths on your property, further endangering you."

Tears flowed down my cheeks and I didn't bother to wipe them away. I'd managed to clear my parents' names and in the process discovered that all of us had been duped by a con artist for years.

Hal was staring at me as if there was more he wanted to say. I sighed. "If you want to tell me something, Hal, please just say it. I'm too tired to guess."

"Devon Little put you in danger by first stealing that painting and then leaving it here for the last two years. And he turned you into bait so we'd take care of Heather Masterson for him. You could have been killed. Caphy was badly hurt..."

I blinked, realizing he was right. Dev had endangered my dog with his shenanigans. It would be a long time before I forgave him for that. "He did. You're right. He made some really poor choices."

"Like your father."

I flinched. He'd hit me right in the bullseye of my broken heart. "I don't want to talk about my dad right now."

"Your dad knew Heather was unstable. He knew someone had stolen from her. And he just went off and left you behind. She could have come looking for the painting back then. She could have killed you or used you as bait to get it back from him."

I closed my eyes as each of his accusations pierced my closely-held delusions. Tears burned behind my eyelids. I shook my head. "He left me with Uncle Dev. I was protected."

"Were you? I'm not really impressed with *Uncle Dev's* commitment to your well-being."

He was right again. But there had to be more to it. Something we weren't understanding. "He must have had a good reason to leave."

Hal seemed to be biting his tongue. I could tell there was more he wanted to say, but he apparently realized it wouldn't change anything and would only hurt me more. So, he kept his mouth closed and pulled me under his arm, kissing me on the temple as we settled back on the couch.

Several quiet, healing moments passed and I began to relax, enjoying his warmth and the constant support of the man providing it. Even his anger was healing. He was angry *for* me rather than *at* me and I understood that. It was a wonderful thing to have someone care that much again.

"I just have one more burning question," he said a moment later.

I tensed again. "What's that?"

"How did Devon make the grass move like that?"

I grinned, relaxing. "Remote control cars. They were in my dad's office."

"Ah. Ingenious."

"Yeah," I agreed, sighing happily as he pulled me closer. Only a couple of things threatened to ruin the moment. "I miss my dog," I said a moment later.

"I know." He rubbed my arm.

I waited another beat. "You're going to leave now, aren't you? Go back to Indy?"

He didn't respond at first. His big, warm hand kept rubbing my arm as we sat there in companionable silence.

Finally, he gave me a squeeze. "I've got some vacation time coming. How about if I stick around *Deer Hollow* for a while and you can show me all the best tourist traps in the area?"

I smiled, leaning my head against his chest. "I'd like that."

His heart beat slow and strong under my ear. "So would I." He said. "I'd like it a lot, actually."

I lifted my gaze and looked up into his too-handsome face. Our eyes caught and held. Then he slowly lowered his head and touched his lips to mine.

And just like that, all the bad stuff of the last few days drifted away.

At least for a little while.

The End

ALSO BY SAM CHEEVER

If you enjoyed **Humpty Bumpkin**, you might also enjoy these other fun mystery series by Sam. To find out more, visit the **BOOKS** page at www.samcheever.com:

Gainfully Employed Mysteries
Honeybun Heat Series
Silver Hills Cozy Mysteries
Country Cousin Mysteries
Yesterday's Paranormal Mysteries
Reluctant Familiar Paranormal Mysteries

ABOUT THE AUTHOR

USA Today and Wall Street Journal Bestselling Author Sam Cheever writes mystery and suspense, creating stories that draw you in and keep you eagerly turning pages. Known for writing great characters, snappy dialogue, and unique and exhilarating stories, Sam is the award-winning author of 80+ books.

To learn more about Sam and her work, visit her at one of her online hotspots:
www.samcheever.com
samcheever@samcheever.com

CPSIA information can be obtained
at www.ICGtesting.com
Printed in the USA
LVHW031108210320
650785LV00004B/1136